MAN
HANDS

SARINA BOWEN & TANYA EBY

RENNIE ROAD BOOKS

1 SANDWICHES AND SORROW

Brynn

"What you need is to be fucked."

Ashley says this to me, and I sorta can't breathe. The not-breathing is because I'm winded from giving Ash and Sadie a very long monologue about how desperate and alone I feel now that my divorce is final. A divorce I wanted, mind you, but the end of my marriage is devastating.

I've failed at marriage.

My Monologue of Despair was so all-consuming that I haven't even taken a bite out of my crisp, gooey Cuban sandwich with garlicky mojo sauce. That's how bad things really are—I let that slice of salty ham heaven just sit there and get soggy and cold, like my love life.

Because I am in despair.

So after Ash says, "You need to be fucked," I can't breathe. It's partly because my nose is filled with snot over my sorrow, and also because, goddamn it, she's right.

I take a bite of the sandwich, just so, you know, she'll continue with this line of thought.

"...and I'm not talking that kind of 'Oh you complete me' bullshit and 'Can I touch you here' lovey shit. I mean the growling, fumbling, grunting—"

"Biting," Sadie adds as she steals one of my fries.

"—*biting* kind of hot fucking. You know, headboard-knocking fucking. The kind where you're all..."

"Sweaty?" I guess.

"Yes! Sweaty, but that good kind of sex sweat, right? Like when you're done and you're starving and you go to the store for ice cream, people take one whiff of you and they know. They *know!*"

"They know you got the dick," Sadie finishes.

I sort of giggle-burp because I'm really emotional right now and this sandwich is so good, and Sadie, a therapist and a mom to newborn twin girls, isn't one to use the word "dick". Usually, it's penis, if she says anything at all. She's my most anatomically correct friend.

"What I'm saying is—" Ash holds up one finger to mark her place while she drains the rest of her beer. "—stop wallowing and let's find you someone to screw."

I swallow another bite of my sandwich, and then I realize a bearded waiter is leaning over the adjacent table, mesmerized. He's polishing the same few inches of the wood surface over and over again with a dirty gleam in his eye.

Also, he's wearing really tight hipster pants.

That's when me and my friends—my dear friends from college, my soul sisters—share a secret glance of amusement. We're at eye level with his crotch and the evidence therein. He's not our waiter, but it's clear that he'd still like to help us out with anything we want... and not just food and beverages.

Ash leans forward, maybe to get the waiter's attention by hoisting up her boobs, or maybe she just wanted to rest them on the table. "You, sir. I can see you're invested in this conversation. Can I ask you a rather blunt hypothetical question?"

I try to kick her under the table, but I am on my second mojito and the first mojito went straight to my fine-motor skills, meaning I am one mojito away from drooling, two away from peeing.

He blinks, and then he blinks again. He moves his skinny hips closer to the end of our table and I have to avert my gaze. "Hit me. I love this conversation."

"Well then." Ash shoots me a look. "Hypothetically," she asks, "would you fuck my friend? Like, a good fuck? Not a romantic fuck?"

Blink. Blink. Blink. Then: "I'm working a double shift," he says.

"I'm not talking *reality*," Ash scoffs. "I'm talking hypothetically. You know that hypothetically means in the supposed universe, right? As in, *just in theory?*"

He adjusts his pants. There is a marked swelling on one side of his leg, and I can't help but do a double take. That enlargement travels almost to his knee. I mean, it's a fucking *anaconda*. He could jump rope with that thing.

"Sure," he says. "I mean, not that I would, I'm totally engaged to my girlfriend. It's on Instagram and everything. We had chalkboards with our names on it and the date and all. But yeah. I'd totally fuck her." He leans down and whispers, "Against. A. Wall."

There is a pregnant silence, by which I mean I could almost get pregnant just basking in his stare. His eyes are on my generous cleavage. Sometimes I find that sort of behavior from a waiter rude. But he's not our waiter. And since we just invited him to hypothetically boink me, I can't really hold it against him.

Hypothetically.

Sadie snorts, breaking the silence. "Hopefully not these walls," she says, motioning to the wood paneling. "Splinters."

"Ow," he agrees, leaning close to me, and I swear he smells like wonderful things, including bacon. "I get off at three a.m. Just saying."

There is another awkward pause, and I pass the time admiring his trouser snake. I'm a little worried that it's going to bust out of his pants all Hulk-like. Some kind of response is required of me, but mojitos and pheromones have rendered me speechless.

"She's *not* going to be wallbanged by an engaged man," Sadie says, answering for me.

Right. I'm not. I'm not one for casual...wallbanging. I need an emotional connection. I needed someone like...Steve.

Goddamn it!

My emotions suddenly flood me again as I picture Steve. Slender Steve. My husband. My ex-husband. Our first kiss. The first time we made love, and he apologized because he couldn't keep an erection. The last time we made love and...he apologized for not keeping an erection.

Ash snaps her fingers in front of my face. "Stay with us, Brynn! Don't go toward the light!" To the waiter she says, "Check, please!"

He speeds off.

"All right," Ash says, fishing her credit card out of her purse. "What did we just learn?"

"The waiter has an extra limb?" I offer.

"Oh, honey," Sadie says with a sigh. Motherhood has made her a very effective sigher. "Answer this question for me: is that man attractive? I mean—are you attracted to him?"

I think about it before answering. I sip the rest of my mojito until it slurps. I try to analyze the peculiar warmth and throbbing in my vagina. Is it attraction or a urinary tract infection? Hmm.

"Yes. I am attracted to him." I mean, he's skinny and wearing tight pants and has a funky mustache. He looks like he writes poetry and listens to Philip Glass or something. His skin is slightly translucent, even though it's June.

He's totally my type.

"That's what I thought." Sadie grips my hand. Her fingers are cold and so fragile. "As your friend... No, as your therapist, I'm telling you from here on out, if you're attracted to a guy, it's a giant red flag. I agree with Ash that you totally need to be fucked, and we should make this our mission as your friends and sisters by choice. But here's the thing—you *can't* be attracted to the guy. Not at all."

"Wait." I'm having trouble following her, which is probably the mojitos' fault. "You want me to fuck someone unattractive?"

They shake their heads in perfect synchronicity. "No, babe," Ash says. "You need to do the nasty with someone who isn't your type. If your body is responding with all those whozits and whatsits, then you need to run away because your instinct is just plain wrong. You make bad choices."

Sadie is nodding along. "Really bad."

"So..." This can't be a good idea. "You want me to jump back into the dating world, forgetting that my tender emotions have been run through a pasta machine." (I'm a food blogger. Don't judge my metaphors.) "You want me to ignore my instincts? My own body?"

They're nodding. They're totally nodding!

I think of Steve again and when I told him I was leaving him. "Ah," he'd said.

Ah.

I burst into tears.

The waiter brings us the bill and another mojito for me. "On the house," he says and winks. His mustache, I swear, waves.

Ash and Sadie don't say anything. Oh no. They just let me sit for a while. It's loud in here, with the sounds of laughter and carefree Friday night cavorting. But it's all weirdly quiet in my mind. "Okay," I finally say. And then I drink the rest of my mojito in one long, impressive slurp.

I also think I pee a little.

2 MY SPIRIT ANIMAL

Brynn

By now I have tried on a hundred dresses. A hundred!

Okay, four. Still.

With each one it's the same story. Bloated face, huge boobs, hips built to carry three or four children, and anvil feet. How? How did I let this happen to myself? The mirror hates me. It's propped up against the wall because this is a new apartment and I don't know how to do anything, and hanging a mirror is just too much work. But still, something is just wrong.

I grab the edges of the mirror, thinking to give it a little shake. I'd rather shake Steve for wrecking my self-esteem, but he's not available.

It proves unsatisfying to wrestle a mirror, though, so I lean it against the wall again, this time at less of an angle. And when I catch my reflection again, something has shifted. My face is slimmer, my hips less otherworldly. Even my cleavage is perkier.

It's a miracle!

Wait.

Okay, who knew that mirrors can make you look funny when they were angled on the wall? Not me, obviously. I've been in this new house for two months already, wondering how I'd become so stumpy looking. I'd thought it was a side effect of divorce.

So this is a shred of good news, and I've needed that.

Even so, I don't feel like going to a party. I grab my phone and add a message to the three-way text conversation I've had going with my friends for, I swear, whichever year texting was invented.

> **Me: I'm not going.**
> **Ash: Fuck you. You're going.**
> **Sadie: Just wear the wrap dress. The wrap dress is**
> **made for every body shape. The wrap dress can**
> **make the Michelin Man look sexy.**

I'm not sure how Sadie knows I'm struggling with what to wear. Okay, she's a therapist and all. But sometimes her level of empathy puts her in the category of being freaky.

> **Me: I don't want to go. You guys have fun. I think I**
> **have the flu.**
> **Ash: You don't have the flu. You're going.**
> **Me: Ebola. I have Ebola. And you don't joke about**
> **Ebola.**

There's a knock at my door, and I hear Ash screaming, "I'm here! Open the fucking door or I'm going to start fucking swearing!"

Crud. Since I'm new to the neighborhood, I'm worried about what the neighbors will think of their new, psychotic, recently divorced, bloated neighbor, so I throw on the wrap dress, tie it, run downstairs, and open the door.

Ash and Sadie look at me, stunned. "I gotta say," Sadie says, "Exposing your breast like that is really..." She looks like she can't think of the right word.

"Adventurous?" Ash offers.

"Adventurous, yeah, but maybe not..."

"Wise," I finish, looking down to see that I tied the dress, yes, but I left one boob out in the open. Thank god it's covered by my sports bra. Still. This was almost a full-on nipple infraction. In front of the neighbors too. "Get in here," I say and wave them inside.

Ash and Sadie look great. They always do. Ash is a ruthless realtor, ever keen to make the sale. She doesn't take any bullshit, and right now she's dressed like she just barbecued some poor soul and then went shopping at Bergdorf to celebrate. She's sleek and thin and blond, of course, and intimidating as hell.

Sadie, new mom to the cutest babies on the planet, is softer, with wispy, curly brown hair, brown skin, and eyes that make you want to bake her a muffin. Ash is in a pencil skirt and a silky blouse thing, and Sadie has on this bohemian kind of dress that shows off her clavicles and I'm pretty sure she's braless.

And I'm wearing a too-tight dress with my sports-bra boob hanging out. No wonder Steve couldn't get it up for me.

Right then and there, I start to cry.

"I can't go out on the prowl, guys. I don't want to do this. Too scary," I whine. "I just want to cook something and post it online and have a thousand people like it so I feel validated. Can't I do that instead?"

"No," they say.

Fucking girlfriends.

Ash runs past me, heading upstairs. "Where are you going?" I call after her skinny butt.

"You are not wearing granny underwear and a sports bra!" she calls back.

How does she know about the underwear? They're comfortable. I used to reserve them for when I had my period, but that seemed silly. Why not wear them every day? The same *kind* of gigantic panties. Not the same pair, because *ew*.

"What you wear against your skin affects how you present yourself on the outside," Sadie offers. "Right now, I'm totally naked underneath." I take a longer look at her. She is. Naked as can be under all her clothes, her breasts round and heavy. Must be the babies.

"Don't you...uhm...chafe?" I ask, glancing down a bit.

"I put lotion on my labia majora. It's fine."

I nod, as if I know exactly where that is. I'm a writing professor, not a biologist. And the labia majora doesn't crop up too often in my students' essays. But maybe it should.

Actually, I *was* a writing professor. Now I'm jobless. My ex's father is the chair of the English department where I worked. I got a pink slip in the mail the day after I signed my divorce papers.

"I'm unemployed," I say, trying out the word. It sounds just as bad out loud as it did inside my head.

"I know, baby." Sadie pats me on the hand. "But it's Saturday and we're going to get you drunk and then laid. Get with the program."

From upstairs comes the sound of thumping, and drawers opening. Then the closet door opening. I could go up there and help her look, give some guidance, but I honestly have no energy. Standing is hard. Breathing takes an act of will.

Going to this party? That's an act of god that I just don't see happening.

I can hear the tear of cardboard as she rips open one of my moving boxes. Then a gasp. "You have the worst lingerie I've ever seen!"

I'm relieved. For a minute there, I worried that I'd packed some poor woodland creature in my haste to get out of my marriage, and didn't notice.

"You can wear these tonight, but we are going shopping tomorrow!" She's coming down the stairs, a look of pure determination on her face. "You need to treat yourself better, Brynn!"

She throws a black bra and pink panties at me. The panties were a gag gift from Ash herself, this past Easter. They say *Chocolate Bunnies Are My Spirit Animal*, and they're printed all over with—wait for it—chocolate bunnies. They're ridiculous, and yet still a step up from what I'm currently wearing.

At the time I'd left him, Steve hadn't shown any interest in me in over a year. Hence, the grannie panties. After a while, I'd given up. Why bother being sexy for a man who doesn't even see you? Unless I was serving him a plate of food, I was invisible to him. Like, I could literally be in a room and he'd turn off the light because he didn't know I was there. Lingerie was just an invitation for humiliation.

These are my thoughts as Sadie unwraps my dress and slides it off me, because I'm not humiliated enough yet.

"You can change in front of us. It's no big deal," she says and I'm too tired to fight with her. "I've had a whole group of people staring at my vagina and it's really not an issue. Especially when you're in labor."

Sadie whips off the gigantic bloomers and the sports bra. She's good at this. It must be all that diaper changing.

I wiggle into the bra and chocolate-bunny underwear on my own power. And I have to admit, I feel about five pounds lighter. Sadie fastens the dress around me, mercifully covering both boobs this time, and adjusts. "You. Are. Gorgeous," she says. I grunt. Then she grabs my face and forces me to look at her. "You. Are. Gorgeous. Okay?"

"Ohh-kaw," I say, because she's got a hold of my jaw. She loosens her grip. "Let's just go. Let's get this over with."

"That's the spirit." Ash gives me an evil grin.

"What exactly is happening tonight?" I ask Ash as she heads for the door. They'd told me earlier, but I was too grumpy to listen.

"We're going to a party my competitor is throwing. He's a total dicknozzle but he makes a ton of money and supposedly throws killer parties."

"If you hate him, why are we going?" I ask. Maybe I can weasel out of this yet.

"To see his mansion and drink his alcohol!" Ash yelps. "Duh."

"And admire his cute, rich friends," Sadie adds.

"This house is on Reeds Lake," Ash informs me. That's a fancy-shmancy little lake in a decadent neighborhood. So my interest in this party goes from zero to, say, one and a half. "And there will be live music and free booze and lots and lots and lots of men."

"Is your colleague gay?" I ask hopefully. I don't want tonight to be all about finding me a hookup. Merely surviving the party is enough of a challenge for the newly divorced.

"He was in a fraternity. Or something. Whatever. We're going and while we're there, we are going to help you find someone to flirt with."

"Someone you're not attracted to," Sadie reminds me. "Because red flag."

"Because my instincts are wrong," I agree.

"Totally wrong. And that's okay. It's fixable. But we'll find someone who's the exact opposite of your type."

"Explain your type again." Ash says. "Let's define the problem."

I squint my eyes, because everyone knows that makes you smarter. I didn't know I had a type, but when I look back on my few exes over the years...yeah. There seems to be a pattern. "Frail looking. Vegetarian or gluten free. Intellectual. Ironic. Good hygiene."

Sadie and Ash just look at me for a beat. "Thank god we're helping you," Ash says. "I mean...what the fuck? Why didn't we notice this before?"

Sadie is nodding.

Ash says, "So we just need to find someone who's huge, a carnivore, doesn't talk..."

"Smells manly and... What's the opposite of ironic?"

"I have no idea. Let's simplify it—we're looking for a *man* instead of what you've been attracted to."

"What have I been attracted to?"

"Gwyneth Paltrow, I'm pretty sure. And every time I see her on TV, I just want to kick her."

Sadie is still nodding. "It's true. You have to move on from the sensitive pseudodudes. You need to find a..."

"Cock," they say at the same time.

I can't help but smile. I mean, come on. These two. Maybe they are my act of god.

3 TOP TEN

Brynn

Things I Felt While In My Marriage, And Why I Wanted Out:

1. In the beginning we were filled with hope, then we were just tired.
2. We were married for seven years. He never remembered our anniversary, my phone number, or that I hate raw onions.
3. I wanted to have kids. He wanted a hamster.
4. My sex drive increased over the years. His libido shrunk. I found comfort in food and started my food blog. I gained weight. Sex was something we scheduled and he tended to as if fucking me was akin to cutting an ingrown toenail.
5. He never fucked me. He scheduled time for us to "be intimate."
6. I started to hate the way he chewed, how he smelled, how his eyebrows were overgrown, the way he said "pasta."
7. I started to disappear and he didn't even notice.
8. I didn't feel loved or cherished or wanted. I felt like I was a constant mistake.
9. When I looked in the mirror, I stopped being able to recognize myself.

10. He had an ugly penis.

That last one might be a little mean. Still. It was sorta ugly. It had a big vein and it curved in a way that seemed like he was built to actively turn away from my g-spot. But really, the list doesn't mean squat. The only truth that really matters is this:

1. I just didn't love him anymore, and I didn't even love myself.

4 LUSH WILLOWS AND FLOWERING SHRUBBERIES

Brynn

We're in East Grand Rapids. This is the posh part of Western Michigan, where people are well-groomed and play lacrosse and have kids named Denver and Saurin and Blade. Seriously. Sadie has a teacher friend whose first-grade class last year had a Blade G. and a Blade P. It's unsettling.

The dicknozzle's house is tucked off Lake Drive. There's a giant iron gate that lets you know you don't belong here, and I'm already convinced it's true. Maybe they won't even let us in.

There are shiny, beautiful cars on the cobblestone driveway. The hedges are trimmed. It's a sultry July night and the breeze blows off the lake, making everything rustle. And there are lights everywhere. I hear music too. It's like walking into some Hollywood backlot, only this is real.

"Ash," I whisper as we climb out of the cab. I say *Ash* the way I'd say it if we were in a horror movie and she wanted to check out the dark basement and see what that strange growling noise is. She is, actually, named after the dude in *The Evil Dead*, so this seems appropriate.

"It's totally fine," she says. "We'll have drinks and then we won't even notice how douchey everyone is."

It suddenly occurs to me that I'm taking advice from the wrong friend. Ash's love life isn't going so well. Her ex is in prison, for starters. And, instead of putting herself out there in the way she's urging me to, she's invented a boyfriend named Hunter so her parents will stop asking questions. I haven't really understood this approach, but that's okay. With Ash, you have to just go with it.

But now my objections rise up inside me like a bad case of gas. I glance around, looking for the best shrubbery to hide behind. But before I get the chance to dart away, the apparent owner of this monstrous house has appeared. He's caressing Ash. Maybe it's some kind of hug, but this guy hugs her the way amoebas blend into one another. It's kind of gross, but also mesmerizing.

"And who do we have here?" he asks, looking at me and Sadie. Mostly Sadie.

But Sadie's oblivious. It's strange. She's incredibly insightful and empathetic, and then there are times when I wonder if anyone is home in her brain. Or maybe she's relieved to have an hour and a half free of being suckled by her babies. Or maybe she's just thinking of how much she's in love with her husband who is out of town right now visiting his mother who just had surgery. Her husband has a high libido, and she once told us that they do it every day.

If I had that, I'd be a little dreamy too.

Ash introduces us this way: "Braht, these are my friends. You can't touch them. Can we have some drinks now." She doesn't phrase it as a question.

I shake my head, wondering if I heard his name correctly. No. His name can't really be Braht. Like bratwurst? Who has a name like that?

Braht snaps his fingers. He actually fucking snaps and a waiter appears with three drinks on a tray.

And, omigod, it's a sign! The drinks are served in pineapples, with a banana garnish that's carved to look like a dolphin. The dolphin has a little cherry in its adorable little mouth. "Omigod!" I squeal. "I love tiki drinks!"

Braht visibly swells with pride. Not in his pants like our poor waiter—he gets big in a rooster-chested way. "I hired Beachbum Berry to prepare our drink menu! He's totally famous. A real icon. And his drinks—they'll get you absolutely *hammered*." Braht reminds me of James Spader in *Pretty In Pink*. The slimy rich boy. And damn if it doesn't make Braht sort of likable.

"Nice," I say, helping myself to a pineapple. The night is looking up. Except that I can't breathe all of a sudden. Panic attack, maybe? Or maybe my wrap dress is really tight. It *is* really tight. "I can't breathe," I complain. Sadie nods, undoes my dress and re-ties it. Right there in front of Braht.

"Lovely," he says. I can't tell if he's being ironic or not.

Ironic! Red flag! At least my well-intentioned friends won't try to steer me toward a tryst with Braht. That's a relief because I'd be thinking about bratwurst the whole time. How awkward.

"We'll see you later," Ash says to Braht, dismissing him. It makes me love her just a little bit more, that she can come to some rich dude's party and treat him like he owes her something.

On second thought, maybe he does? I turn around and he's watching us walk away with an expression of...longing? Then he shakes himself and straightens his spine. He calls "Hello, Edelweiss!" to a woman with perfect, shiny hair. She's wearing a silver tube top that cost more than my college education.

She turns to him with a grin, and her sparkly chest catches the light. I want to poke my eyes out with a fork.

Ash tugs on my hand and leads the way. The house is all marble floors and shiny things. I want to stop and admire the kitchen. It's just the sort of chef's paradise I've always wanted. Over the sink there's a gleaming faucet as large as St. Louis's Gateway Arch.

But Ash is on a mission, and she tows me toward the oversized back patio. 1950s Hawaiian music is playing, and, against every molecule of my being, I actually like this place.

We walk down some brick steps and into a garden area with lush willows and flowering shrubs. Everything is balanced and beautiful and I don't really understand how it's even possible to achieve such perfection. When Braht snaps his manicured fingers, the plants must leap to do his bidding.

"Wow," Ash says as the three of us look around. I see a look of awe cross her face. But less than a second later she catches herself, shaking it off. With a shrug she says, "Bottoms up!"

And we sip, sip, sip that pineapple until the drinks are gone. They're really terrific too. Fruity, rummy, and cinnamony. Or something. I should really write a blog post about them. They're perfectly photogenic.

But ambition slips away as Ash hands me another drink that magically appears, and we sip, sip, sip one more time.

Then everything goes black.

No it doesn't. I just blinked for a really long time.

Although, things do start to get weird. There must be a glitch in the Matrix, because of all people in the universe, I think I see Steve standing with a small group of people across the yard. I blink twice and then look again. Sure enough, my ex-husband has an arm wrapped around a very tall, very young, very thin redhead and...

I sort of lose my shit.

5 SHEER PROPULSION

Brynn

I think I'm hyperventilating. Really. My breath comes in rhythmic, soft grunts that are more primal than sexual. I don't know what that means.

That's not true. I do know what it means. It's the sound of shock.

Because Steve's hand is slowly pulling the girl closer to him, and then that hand goes creeping down her ass.

Worse, the girl is sort of like the photo-shopped version of...me. Our coloring is the same, but she's taller and thinner and *younger* with fewer blemishes. She also glows, probably from buffing. And it's not fair. It really isn't! I'd glow too if I did some buffing.

Why the fuck haven't I been buffing?

The crowd they're standing with can't see Steve's butt-cheek maneuver, but I can see it perfectly. It's a secret message he's sending, and I've heard the broadcast loud and clear: my ex-husband is fucking a beautiful, thin, younger woman. My ex-husband *never* laid his hand on my ass like that, never publicly claimed me that way.

My ex-husband didn't have a problem with his libido. He just had a problem getting freaky with *me*.

"Uh-oh," Sadie says. Maybe she sees the tears forming in my eyes about to cascade down my face, or maybe she senses the seismic shift that is happening within me. I'm grunting and I'm vibrating, and not in a good way. Maybe, just possibly, I'm going to self-combust because of pain. "Ash?" Sadie says with more than a little panic in her voice. "Do something!"

"What's wrong—" Ash inhales sharply as she sees the spectacle over yonder. "Fuckfuckfuck," she says. "Quick. Brynn. Take a deep breath. You're not breathing. Breathe." She spins me so I'm looking at her. "Do not take your eyes off me, okay? You can get through this. You can dance through this beautifully. And you know how you're going to do that?" She doesn't wait for me to answer. "In a minute, I'm going to release you, and you are going to do something totally out of character. You're going to do what I tell you to do. Do you hear me? *Do you?*"

This time it isn't rhetorical. I grunt in response.

"Sadie, your drink," Ash snaps.

Sadie swaps her full pineapple for my empty one. "Suck it down," she orders. And I do. I suck for all my worth. This is liquid courage and, by god, I need it.

I'm staring at Ash like she's the only thing securing me to earth, and maybe she is. Her voice is calm but authoritative. I have known her for fifteen years, and I trust her with my life. So when she says, "You're going to do what I tell you to do," I just nod. I nod because I'm hurt and confused and fucking lonely and lost and oh...wait a minute...that feels nice....I'm a little bit drunk.

Ash squeezes my shoulders. "Okay. When I spin you around, I want you to run and kiss the first guy that makes eye contact."

I squeak a little.

"Don't question me right now, bitch! This is serious. You are going to do this or we aren't friends. You hear me?"

I'm not sure the threats are really all that encouraging, but I don't care, because listening to her is keeping me from going full-on insane over my ex and his happy fingers.

"And...now!" She grabs the pineapple from my hands and spins me around. Then she slaps my ass. Hard.

And I do it! I charge out of the gate like I'm a possessed stallion at the Kentucky Derby. I don't even spare a glance toward Steve. I just take off running. I think I'm even screaming. It's like

"Yieyieyieyieyie!" Or something. And I'm running as fast as my sturdy thighs can propel me.

The people around me are a mélange of hipsters and yuppies. Since I'm running, they blur together, becoming yupsters.

Whatever. They don't matter, because I'd be attracted to whatever a yupster is. They're probably all vegans and sensitive and That Is A Red Flag. So I go against my natural instincts, and zero in on the guy crouching down in the terraced garden and planting a bush. The gardener! Perfect!

Miraculously he stands up, like I somehow commanded him to. Maybe I did. It's hard to say because I'm fucking insane right now. One look at him and I *know* he eats meat. He may be the fucking gardener, but he's got arms like a linebacker. He's wearing a baseball cap over a perfectly weathered face.

He's pushing forty, maybe, and he looks like he's lived outside under the sun, or has at least visited the outdoors once in a while.

And he just looks...like a man. All six feet whatever inches of him. Our eyes lock and I fucking launch myself at him, like a rocket! I mean, with my weight and the sheer propulsion of my body, a tackle from me should send him flying edge of the terraced gardener and straight into the lake. But the dude catches me. He. Catches. Me. And he squeezes my ass!

Although, to be fair, the ass squeeze might be the only thing keeping me from hurtling over the balcony.

But I don't analyze it, because I'm already on to the next part of my mission. His lips are full, and I attach mine to them like a barnacle in heat. And then I'm sucking off his face like some possessed vacuum cleaner.

For a moment, I'm the only one sucking. That would have gotten embarrassing pretty fast, but a beat later my gardener gets the memo. His brawny arms lock around my body. He shifts me higher on his body, and my legs naturally wrap around his waist. Like it was meant to be.

And that generous mouth deepens the kiss.

Seriously, it's better than bacon. Firm lips conquer mine. One of his big hands tightens on my ass, and the other...the other hand goes into my hair and he *tugs it a little*. Dear god. He was kissing *me* with more heat than

I thought possible outside a movie studio. A manly sound comes from somewhere deep in his chest, and he holds me so close I think we could maybe withstand a tornado. I melt into him, like a good fondue cheese.

And this is why I should never have more than two drinks. Because I almost pee a little.

6 THE GARDENER

Tom

Now, here's the thing. I've been a TV personality for over ten years, and I have seen some freaky shit. I once pulled down a wall that was humming to find a hive with a billion bees in it. I'm not joking—it was like some Saturday night horror movie. And I've fallen through rotted floor boards. Twice.

But this strange episode developing in front of me is so much more interesting.

I feel the woman running before I actually see her. There I am, crouching down to give the new lilac a good start in the earth, when I felt a great thudding. I don't know what makes me rise as if to meet my destiny. But when I do, I see this demon woman charging toward me.

It's hard to see the whole picture at once, because there's a lot of motion. Full breasts rising and falling a surprising distance from the force of her running. She's wrapped up in some kind of dress thing, and the breeze causes it to flap open, giving me a nice glimpse of what that dress is trying to cover up.

Wowza, my dick says, forgetting everything we've accomplished these past few months. *Come to daddy*.

Crazy fans are nothing new to me. When my show is filming, they crop up everywhere. I've even been accosted in the airport by a screaming horde of women so delirious over seeing me that a few of them cried. One fainted. They stop me to tell me which episode was their favorite—like the one where I waded through wet cement to hold up a falling wall with my body while a tornado whipped unexpectedly through a Texas town.

But I have never...in all those years...experienced something as thunderous as this. Literally. The earth is shaking beneath me.

And then I look into her green eyes and everything goes into slow motion. They're a beautiful color. Like Benjamin Moore's Clearspring Green. Even better, need is burning in her gaze. And it's *me* she needs. I know she's going to leap. I can just feel it.

Over my ten years as a host for *Mr. Fixit Quick*, I've had my share of crazy moments. You'd think I'd learn that when a body in motion comes charging toward me, I'd have the sense to maybe *step out of the way*.

But noooooo. Nope. No. I brace myself like I'm back in high school, and I'm a defensive back. I see her coming, and I'm like, *"Fuck yeah. I've got this, coach."*

And I do. She leaps. I see it in slow motion and I think, *"Right here, baby, I got you."* My arms snap closed at just the right time. She is...she's sorta heavy...but I'm prepared. Every muscle in me locks up tight, and I hoist her up in the air.

Then she wraps her legs around me, and it's what I imagine it feels like to be squeezed by a python, if you were sexually attracted to a python, because she squeezes me hard with her legs and I feel her enormous breasts pushed against my body, and her ass in my hands, and I gotta tell you, I like it, I like it a whole lot, and she's suddenly kissing the life out of me, and it's all I can do to just hold on.

So I do. I hold on. I dig my hands into her ass, and I hold her there. And before I really know what's happening, her crazy-ass kiss lights a fire inside me. Suddenly, I'm kissing her too, and everything slows down a bit more. She tastes like cinnamon, and I forget about the fucking party and fucking Braht and his dumbass ideas, and all I can think is: *I need this woman underneath me and naked, and I need this to happen in about five minutes.*

Maybe less.

So that's when I start walking with her wrapped around me like a squid. And I can't get enough of her.

This is not good.

This is SO good.

It's both at once.

I promised my agent—and myself—that I'd stay away from women. A year of celibacy. That was my plan.

But hey, plans change.

We are locked together like eels as I carry her down to the boathouse and kick open the door. I don't know why she flew onto my body and attached herself to me. But I haven't felt this alive for months. Maybe ever. And I've never felt more fucking male than I do right now.

7   I LOVE HARDWOOD

Brynn

I have entirely lost my mind. It's somewhere on Braht's pretty lawn, beneath a willow tree.

And good riddance. I don't care that I've lost my mind, because I've found my vagina. My poor neglected vagina that's been ignored for so very long. In fact, all of me has been ignored for so very long that it takes me a few moments to realize that I am wrapped around a perfect stranger.

The gardener breaks our kiss for a second, and I realize that I'm in a room. A garage? I take a quick look, and I see a sailboat that someone's working on. It's all sleek and shiny. There's the smell of paint or turpentine and man. I really don't know anything about boats, but even I can tell this one looks expensive. It must be, because it's made of hardwood.

I love hardwood. Speaking of which...

There's a man standing between my legs, and I'm sitting propped on a pile of cushy boat seats, and I'm panting.

"Hi," he says. One word and I can tell he has the voice of pure sex. Sex and testosterone and probably bullfighting or something. He's no Steve, that's for sure. And then he smirks. It's the cutest fucking smirk I've ever seen, so I just lean in and kiss it. He hasn't shaved in a few days or maybe this is his natural state, I don't know, but he's a little sandpapery. I need to be smoothed down. I really do.

Then I realize I didn't answer him. Where are my manners? I pull away and I say—actually I just sort of breathe it—"Oh. Hi!"

We stare at each other for a beat. And then he's kissing me again, and I'm back on the stack of cushy seats, and my legs are wrapped around him, pulling him in close like I'm reeling in a big fish.

He reaches for the ties on the side of my dress, and then he stops kissing me and says, "May I?"

May I? What gardener talks like that? What *human* talks like that? I nod eagerly. His muscled arm gives one quick pull, and the bow loosens and my wrap dress is no longer wrapping me because he's pushed it wide open, exposing all of me to the hungriest gaze I've ever seen.

Another sound is tugged from his chest. It's soft and low and needy. We're so close together that I feel the vibration against my lady parts. The room swims a little. I'm so far out of my element it's not even funny.

Thank god I'm not wearing the grannie panties and the sports bra! (I love you, Ash!)

He leans over me, and I arch up, looking for another kiss. But his mouth lands on my neck instead. I move my chin, giving him permission, and I'm not disappointed. He drops eager, open-mouthed kisses down the underside of my jaw, and then trails them down my neck.

I'm vibrating again at the very first one. It's been a million years since anyone worshiped me like this. He dips lower, his tongue skimming the swells of my breasts. He makes this little "uhng" grunt. It's a deep grunt. A grunt that would certainly make me have an erection if I had a penis. I feel *something*, and I think I'll call it a ghost erection. Man, am I hung! And I arch a little more.

Somewhere in the back of my consciousness a few of my brain cells attempt a moment of clarity. I'm vaguely aware that I am hardcore making out with a man I just attacked in the garden of a stranger's house while my ex played hand paddle with some beautiful college girl.

But clarity is overrated. And carpe gardener.

I grab this man's hand and put it right on my bra-clad tit. He makes another noise of approval and cups my breast. *YEAH!* I hope I didn't yell that. But it really doesn't matter. The only thing that matters at this very moment is his man-paw and my nipple underneath that fabric.

This is happening. This is real. I can't breathe. I don't even want to.

8 THANKS, MAN

Tom

I had a brain, but it paused for a commercial break about five minutes ago.

This is not part of my regularly scheduled programming. But all I can do is kiss this woman and her beautiful round body and the rise of her glorious tits. I sort of want to plant my face in there and root around for something. Christ.

I can't stop kissing her. I want more than just kisses, but my brain is broken. My hands wander artlessly over her soft skin. I had just enough mental power to ask her permission, and when she granted it, I could only plunge.

Plunge is an apt word. I really want to...

Yeah.

So far, it's just my hands moving over her curves. God, what fucking curves. My ex-girlfriend was so skinny that it was like trying to have sex with a stack of twigs. I was always afraid I'd snap her into pieces. When you want to fuck someone, you don't want to worry about breaking her in half. You want her to be able to take you. All of you.

This woman, though? Fuck. She's a *woman*. She's solid, in the best way a person can be solid. And there's plenty for me to hold on to.

She lifts her body toward mine, her tongue finding my neck, and I just go for it. I reach behind her and—with more tugging than a man who's good with his hands should need—I unhook her bra. Several more of my hard-earned brain cells go up in smoke as I watch her breasts tumble free.

Holy bazongas, Batman.

This is probably a fever dream. Maybe I gave in and drank one of Braht's designer drinks and got loopy. This can't be real. All this perfect boobage in front of me, free for the taking into my mouth. And I fucking do it. My tongue is all over her, taking her nipple against my tongue and sucking until it puckers.

The breathy sounds she makes are driving me crazy. I'm a fucking animal. Maybe it's the six months without dating. Maybe it's the meditation and the yoga Braht's made me do. Maybe I've been working too hard on this house.

Or maybe it's just that this woman is the answer to a wish I hadn't known I'd made.

She pushes my head up and away from her breasts, and I worry that I've gone too far. Could I have missed her signals to stop? That's something I'm serious about getting right.

But then she echoes me. "May I?" she asks.

I look down to find she's got her hands on my belt. I nod or I grunt or whatever. She starts to unfasten the belt. But I'm still wearing more than she is, and that's just not fair. So I peel my T-shirt off and toss it aside. My shorts are next.

I need her underneath me. My heart thuds with excitement because I'm pretty sure where this is headed, and I can't believe my luck.

A year of celibacy just became one hundred forty-seven days of celibacy. But whatever.

"Here," I say, and I pick her up, grab a cushion from the patio furniture that's stored in here, and lay it on the floor. Then I lay her on top of it. I kneel down, one knee on either side of her, straddling her as she looks up at me with giant eyes.

She takes a deep breath. Then her gaze travels my body slowly, descending like an elevator. When she focuses on my abs, she makes a little gurgle of delight. And then her eyes lower further. I look down to see what she sees.

I'm pitching a major tent in my boxers. It's not a budget-sized tent. This tent could house an army unit. So I shift the straining elastic, setting my erection free, kicking off my boxers.

Thanks, man, my dick says.

"No problem, buddy." I'm actually talking to my dick aloud. Whoops. I'm blaming the full moon or the pheromones my lady is letting off. She's staring up at me now, and not with hesitation. I run a palm down my abs and she licks her lips.

Then I take myself in hand while she watches.

That's when her eyes roll back in her head.

9 NICE TO MEET YOU

Brynn

Is swooning a real thing? Because I think it just happened.

One minute I'm watching Mr. Hot get naked. And he is fucking huge. And *beautiful*, which is more surprising. I've never seen a beautiful penis before. Most of them are kinda alien. This one, though...this one...I just want to put it in my mouth. Or in some other part of me. Any part, really.

But then, when he touches himself, it short-circuits my brain. Wires melt up there, or something. The next thing I know, he's kneeling over me, stroking my cheek. "Are you okay?"

"Perfectly," I slur. And it's not the alcohol. I'm getting a contact-high off him.

He kisses me tenderly just once. But then he groans a little and begins rolling my nipples between his lips. One nipple at a time, of course.

When his hips press against mine, I push up to meet him. I'm rubbing myself against him like a cat in heat. The only thing standing between us and the Big Deed is my little pair of Easter panties.

I feel like begging for it, but I don't. That would be unladylike.

He pulls my nipple into his mouth again. Then—thank the lord—his big hand reaches down to trace the seam of the bunny underwear.

"Yes," I breathe, trying to encourage him. *Just do it, Mister!*

He threads his fingers beneath the fabric, and I practically shout with joy. When he hits the spot, I'm embarrassingly wet.

"Oh, fuck yes," he mutters.

"Exactly!" I babble, and then moan as he circles my clit with a thick finger.

"I've got a condom," he rasps. "In my wallet. Like a teenager."

"Yes," I agree. *Finally. Let's go.*

"I want to fuck you," he says, and I nearly swoon again. Nobody ever speaks to me like that. *I freaking love it.* "Right here and right now, but I need to know you're on board."

I nod like a bobblehead doll, lifting my hips for more of his star-studded treatment. Emphasis on stud.

"Baby, you've got to say it."

"I'm good! I want you to. I want you to, you know…" I'm not used to asking for (or getting) what I need. Who knew saying it out loud was so difficult? But I've come this far. I take a deep breath and use all my oxygen to say it. "FUCK ME!"

Every party guest probably heard that. His eyes widen, and, for a horrified second, I worry that I've blown it. But then he smiles. "Yes, ma'am."

Yes, ma'am. My heart pitter-patters. Such manners on my gardener.

Then my brain melts again as he reaches down and rewards me for my bravery with a slow stroke of my pussy. He leans over and *bites my panties off my body.* With his teeth. I didn't even know that was possible.

This is crazy. I know it, I know it, I know it. Still, my brain needs to shut up and let my body enjoy this. It sure doesn't *feel* wrong. Everything feels just right. Especially as his large hand nudges my knees apart.

"Hurry," I say. I don't know why. It just seems imperative that we do this here and now and keep doing it until we both explode.

He's found the condom and unwrapped it already. He starts to roll it down over his dick. But I stop him in order to take over. I have a whole new appreciation for hardwood, because that's what he is. Hard wood. I roll the condom over him. He grits his teeth and thrusts into my hand, and the heated look on his face makes my insides quiver.

Nobody has ever looked at me the way he is right now. I'm

holding my breath again, because I'm afraid to ruin this perfect moment.

He leans down to kiss me again. It's so very sweet and polite. But I'm done with polite. I want him to bite me and squeeze and make the headboard bang into the wall. Except there is no headboard. So I'll just have to settle for regular banging.

He lines up (finally!) and, with an exhale, he eases in. He just keeps easing. For hours, I think. It takes a long, wonderful time.

He bottoms out with a manly grunt, and we are both still. For a minute everything stops. I can hear the lake in the distance and the music from the party. I can hear laughter. The boathouse smells of wood and turpentine and his musk. I can even smell the earth he was digging in. He is inside me, and he fills me in a way that I didn't know I needed.

Then he moves. Just a bit. It's too much and too little. A slow circle. A slight thrust. I run my heels down his ass and give him a tiny shove. I don't want slow. I want to be shattered. "Fuck me," I say, softly at first and then with more force because it feels good to say what I want.

Who knew?

I'm rewarded with another smile. Seriously, a girl could fall hard for that smile. He has big brown eyes that crinkle at the edges.

When he begins to move in earnest, though, the smile falls away. His thrusts are serious work. I hug my knees against his sides and breathe into the motion. He's overwhelming. His tongue strokes across mine, and my synapses can't even absorb all the sensation.

It's...

It's...

I'll get back to you. Words...

Ungh.

We are two bodies, slapping and sweaty and thrumming. It shouldn't be this easy with a stranger. It shouldn't, but I can feel my climax edging closer. It feels like the best kind of being alive, this being whole and desired and wrecked by this man.

I don't want it to ever end. But I can't hold it off anymore. "I'm going to..." I start. But then he grunts and clenches and I can feel his dick spasm within me. Impossibly, the sound of all that masculine power tips me over the edge. With him. It's like a blast of white heat and light, and I clench my muscles so hard that the room goes blurry.

Wow. I feel spent, but also luminous.

We cling to each other, catching our breath. It takes a while for the world to start up again. We're still joined, and I don't want him to ever leave. But admittedly, it would be hard to walk around like this. Go shopping. Eat a sandwich.

He pulls out and collapses next to me. His leg is over mine, and he reaches across my naked breast to grab my hand. "I'm Tom," he says.

"Brynn," I breathe back.

"Well, Brynn... It's really nice to meet you."

We shake hands.

10 ONE LONG WEEK LATER

Tom

This is getting ridiculous. Braht thinks so too. He's frowning at me from across the breakfast table.

It's been a week since I had that woman under me in the boathouse and all I can think about is that woman under me in the boathouse.

No—that's not quite true. I also think of her tits in my mouth, of my hands cupping her everywhere, of the way she kissed me like she was dying for breath and I was air. I even think of her name: Brynn. Brynn. Brynn. It's become a little bit of a mantra in my head, and I am starting to creep myself out.

I'm thirty-eight years old, and I have had some sexual adventures in my life. Literally, adventures. I've been all over the world doing *Mr. Fix It Quick* episodes for H&G, with long breaks in between filming where I may have hooked up with one or two or four local women, but none of those memories has ever stuck with me like my night with Brynn.

Braht slams his hand on the table. "Stop it!" he says. "You're all mopey, and it's fucking distracting."

We're at Wolfgang's Restaurant trying to have a civilized breakfast. I have ordered the Meat Lovers Scrambler and Braht has ordered dry toast and poached eggs. Times like these, I really question his manliness. I also question why he insists everyone call him Braht. I might change my last name too, if my family was as reviled as his.

Not to Braht, though. Braht is the worst name I've ever heard.

But I digress.

"I'm sorry," I say half-heartedly. "I can't stop thinking about her. I mean that was...that was..." I don't have the words for it. The urgency. The heat. It shorted out my brain, and I don't have a lot of extra room in my attic in the first place.

"It's like you were starring in a live porno. You, playing the part of the gardener. Her, the hot, lonely partygoer."

"I'm not the gardener."

"She doesn't know that."

"We think. We *think* she didn't know that," I say.

Braht gives me a look.

I actually hope he's right that she doesn't know who I am. Because that would give her an excellent excuse for not calling me, or at least leaving a business card somewhere conspicuous.

"How is it that you let this perfect creature escape without giving you her last name, anyway?" my best friend asks. "You're always so polite. You usually get the chick's whole life story before any banging happens."

"Usually," I agree. Maybe that's why it was so spectacular this time. Raw. Authentic. Mind blowing. "Afterward, she disappeared like Cinderella at midnight." I'd ducked into the bathroom to ditch the condom, and when I got back she was just...gone. "I don't know how lucid I could have been in that moment. I barely finished a sentence for three days afterward." The sex was really that good.

"Damn," Braht says.

"Damn," I agree.

"Too bad your Cinderella didn't leave a glass slipper." He laughs at his own joke.

"No shoe, nope. But I do have her panties."

He sits up straighter. "You have her panties?"

"Sure do." They're currently in my bedside table. That sounds creepy, but if she'd thought to leave a business card I would've saved that instead.

Braht puts both hands on the table. "Well, there's your clue! If they're unusual, we could find her that way."

"What? No way."

"Way," he says solemnly. "Describe them."

"They're peony pink with an espresso-colored elastic," I say, realizing too late that the precision of this description will make him howl.

And it does.

I wait it out. I can't help having a highly developed color vocabulary. I'm a restorer of fine homes. I own enough paint samples to cover Michigan. "There are chocolate rabbits on the pink underwear," I say when Braht can breathe again. "And a line of text: *Chocolate Bunnies are My Spirit Animal.*"

Braht wipes his eyes and giggles.

"Stop." I kick him under the table. "She's whimsical. She's luscious."

Braht's coffee comes out his nose.

Suddenly, I just can't take it anymore. "That's it! I've got to find her. So why am I sitting here waiting for a Meat Lovers Scrambler with *you?*"

Braht considers this. "First, because you need to eat. You get low blood sugar sometimes and it makes you stressy. Second, you don't even know who this Cinderella is. Third, it's six o'clock in the morning, and, if you went out searching for her now, you'd look like a stalker."

I grunt because it's all true.

"This girl isn't what you need, anyway."

Inside my shorts, my dick begs to differ. "Says you."

"No, I'm serious. You don't need another fuck. You need someone who *knows* you. Your whole self."

My whole self just wants another hour alone with Brynn. "Look, I tried things your way. The yoga. The meditation. My ass fell asleep, and I didn't become enlightened."

He's already shaking his head. "You hold too much back, Tom. You did that with Chandra."

I hiss because he's said my ex's name aloud, and he's not supposed to do that.

"Let me ask you this—did you ever sit her down and tell her about your childhood?"

"Fuck no! Nobody wants to hear about that." My childhood wasn't pretty.

His perfectly shaped eyebrows lift. "You shouldn't even be surprised that it didn't work out with her. She doesn't know you half as well as I do. And you were together for nine months."

I look around, hoping to see the waitress bearing down on our table with the food.

No luck.

"At least tell me this," Braht continues. And I kind of want to kill him. "Did you love Chandra?"

"Sure," I say quickly. *Before she cruelly drop-kicked my heart.*

"Yeah? Tell me the thing you loved best about her. One real thing, and then I won't ask you about her again."

That is a deal I need. So I think hard. I close my eyes and picture Chandra on set at one of our projects together, bending over paint cans while her hair drapes down over the smooth skin of her shoulders. I can't tell Braht how much I liked her hair, because that's not really love. Even I know that.

So I think some more, and it's rough going.

Chandra was the interior designer on *Mr. Fixit Quick*. My sidekick. My gal Friday. And, sure, the on-set romance was Hollywood behavior. I'm not proud. Especially since I was that idiot who thought he'd get a different result than the first thousand victims of show-biz romance.

I loved her because…she was there. And I wanted a person of my very own. My fortieth birthday is less than two years away. The whole bachelor thing is starting to get old.

Crap. That won't fly, either.

After a long silence, I finally realize when I first fell for Chandra —the moment I knew we had something really special.

My eyes fly open. "Episode three!" I say, slapping a hand on the table. "We had a tough assignment. In the center of the living room was a set of antique bookcases—ugly as sin. But the owners insisted on keeping 'em. They put it in the contract and everything. It ruined the feng shui! Then Chandra painted the back of each compartment a different shade of robin's egg blue." I can still see it in my mind. "And it was perfection."

Braht gives me the world's most piteous look.

Luckily, that's when the waitress finally sets my plate in front of me, and I love her a little bit for it. Then I eat a little and, once I feel my blood sugar level out, I'm back to thinking of Brynn. Brynn's eyes. Brynn's breasts. Brynn's hand on my cock.

"You're doing it again!" Braht says.

"What?"

"You're making that mopey face. Stop it. Just fucking find this girl so you can get on with your life."

This is not helpful. "You're the one who threw the party at *my* house. So who is she? Where do I find her?"

"I don't know! There were three hundred people at that party, and I was distracted."

I don't have to ask who the distraction was. It was the realtor babe who works in the Eastown office. He's been in love with her for about five years. She treats him like he's a complete dickwad, and he loves it. He *is* a complete dickwad, most of the time, so I like her for that.

"Give me some details," Braht says and he balances a slice of his poached egg on a tiny end of his toast and takes a dainty bite. I try not to watch.

I think about Brynn's hair instead. It's a soft, silky brown. Feels great between my fingers. And her lips. Plump, full. And that wrap dress I peeled off her. I start to get a little hard at the table, so I eat some Meat Lovers Scrambler to quiet down those endorphins.

Then it occurs to me. What I should do. I grab an extra roll of silverware, unroll it, flatten out the napkin in front of me. "Pen!" I cry.

"Pen? Why?"

"Just hand me a fucking pen!"

Braht hands me a pen. And I draw. I'm inspired. I picture her in my mind, feel my hands rubbing over her curves, and I draw what she looks like. I don't know why I didn't think of this before. It takes me a minute before I triumphantly shove the napkin in his face.

He doesn't say anything for a beat. Then, "You do realize you've drawn a large pair of boobs? It's a nice drawing, Tom. But it's easier to identify a girl by her face."

I'm not sure that's true. But it's no use, anyway. "Ball point on a napkin? I'm good with my hands, but even I couldn't do her face justice. Let's go back to this panty thing. Later I can look at the tag. Would the brand name be any help?"

Braht chews a sad bit of egg. "Hmm. Maybe. But I think the design is more important. What sort of woman wears jokey underwear? She probably has eclectic taste. Lives in Eastown, maybe. Collects vinyl records."

I see where he's going with this. His realtor brain is at work. It's clever, but there's a problem. "I can't just go door to door in Eastown, asking if anyone lost a pair of chocolate bunny underwear. I'll be arrested."

"Maybe," he admits. Then he brightens. "I need a consult! I'll ask for a woman's opinion." He pushes his chair away from the table and takes off running. I mean, he takes off like there's a tsunami coming and he's trying to get to higher ground.

He's forgotten all about me already. This is just an excuse for him to phone up that realtor lady who doesn't give him the time of day and breathe heavily into the phone.

His sad little poached egg sits quivering on his plate. I reach over and pop the thing in my mouth.

Not bad. Not bad at all.

You can't blame me. The fucker took off and left me with the check.

I can only hope that somehow I get in touch with Brynn. And when I say "get in touch with," I mean talk to her, take her out, and then touch her all over. With my tongue.

11 LOOK AT MY SAUSAGE

Brynn

I've placed them next to each other, sort of snuggled together. Thick, golden lengths. I tell Sadie to tilt the collapsible reflector until the light bounces off their tight, glistening shafts just right and—

"For fuck's sake, Brynn! They're sausages! You're taking a picture of meat! This is not high art! Take the picture already so we can eat it!"

Ash has no respect for the intricacies of food photography. The better these sausages look, the more clicks on my site and pins to Pinterest, the more possibility I have of selling one of my cookbooks, the more money I make, the more independent and well-adjusted I feel.

Also, this week I'm obsessed with sausages. Can't think why.

I snap the picture just as Ash lunges and grabs a sausage off the plate, then bites the end off of it.

Bitch.

Sadie grabs the other link.

Motherfucker!

It's a good thing there's an entire pan of bacon too, and they've left alone the quiche and home fries that are just calling my name. I grab my own plate before they can attack again.

Ash really does look like she's ready to attack, and she probably would, if her phone doesn't ring.

She takes a look at the screen. "It's Douchebag," she says. Sadie and I nod. We know who she's talking about. She answers with, "Hi, Douchebag. What do you want?"

Then she walks out of the room. Sadie and I hear her mumbling.

I cut a nice slice of quiche for Sadie, scoop up some extra crispy home fries sprinkled lavishly with herbs and sea salt, and top it all with three pieces of thick-cut bacon, hot from the oven.

Ash can get her own plate. I'm mad at her.

We sit down at my little vintage 1950s metallic kitchen table—the one I bought ten seconds after Steve agreed to a divorce. He always said that vintage was just another word for crap.

I never should have married him.

"How's Decker?" I ask Sadie. I have to wait until she stops moaning for her to answer. She's just taken a big bite of the quiche. It is moanable. I have to say. Basically it's eggs, cream, and cheese. What isn't moanable about that?

"He's good," she finally says. Then she goes back to her plate. There's this weird awkward scraping sound of her fork on the plate. Sadie is usually the one who can read all of us. I'm not as intuitive, but looking at her now, I can feel sadness pouring off her.

"Are you okay?" I ask.

She nods. "Fine. I'm just, I don't know. Tired. Decker..." Sadie's tone is upbeat, but it strikes me as false somehow. Something's...off. I'm not sure how she meant to finish that sentence, but surely it can't be bad. They have sex like every night. Sometimes more than one time a night. That's got to be a sign of a healthy relationship, doesn't it? But then again, that was before they had two little girls to look after. Sadie really does look tired. Usually she's all golden-like, but right now she's a little...tarnished. A little dull. Something is definitely up.

I want to respond to her, I do, but Ash walks back into the room saying, "Okay, fuckwad. I already said okay. Seven p.m. I heard you the first time. Fuck off." That's how she says goodbye. I can feel Braht's lovesick sigh even through the phone. She sits down at the table with us. "That was Braht."

"You don't say?" I ask, and Sadie snorts.

Ash fixes herself a plate. And all the while she takes sneaky little looks at me.

"What?" I finally demand after the fourth or fifth one.

She gives me a shrug. "Let's talk about this gardener of yours."

"There's really no more to say." I'd already spilled the whole story. The kissing and the "May I" and the energetic fucking. The whole thing was so out of character for me I don't think they'd have believed me if they hadn't witnessed the leaping kiss that started the whole event.

"I know how we can find him," Ash says now. Her eyes are sly, and it makes me nervous.

"It wouldn't even be difficult," Sadie says. "We could stake out Braht's house until the landscaper comes by. His phone number will be right on his truck."

I hate this idea. "Who needs the phone number?" I quip. "I could just climb into the truck and do him right there."

"That works for me," Sadie agrees.

"No!" I argue. "It doesn't work at all. I had my fun. I can leave the poor gardener in peace, now."

Ash snickers to herself. "What if he wasn't really the gardener?"

"It doesn't matter," I say, cutting off a giant bite of sausage. If only I could stop thinking about sausage. "His profession isn't the problem."

"Then what is?" Ash asks, sitting up straighter.

"Whrtifhngd?" I try. My mouth is full of sausage. So I make her wait. "What if he's not a good dude? Like—I find my prince again and he's kind of a dick." I have a sneaking suspicion that most men are. "Right now he's perfect, okay? I want him to stay that way."

For a moment, Ash looks troubled. She plays with the teaspoon I've set at her place. This lasts a second or maybe two. Then she brightens up again. "It's fine," she says.

"How is that fine?"

"You leave after the fucking," she says with a shrug.

"There won't be any fucking," I point out.

"Mmh," she says. Either it's a dodge, or she's enjoying my quiche. It could really go either way. "Drinks tonight?" she asks. "I think seven o'clock would be a good time for some tiki drinks, no?"

The subject change is awfully abrupt, and I feel the tiniest prickle of suspicion.

But Sadie brightens up immediately. "I could do drinks. Decker is watching the girls. I tried to get him to call a sitter and go out for dinner with me, but he said he was too tired."

See? Men = dicks.

12 PINING & PUPU PLATTERS

Brynn

I should have been more suspicious when Ash insisted on taking me lingerie shopping that afternoon. And I should have been even *more* suspicious when she insisted that I wear my purchases out of the store. But it saved me from having to unlace the wacky corset thing she'd picked out for me.

And, man, my boobs are so perky! It's like having extra storage space. I could shelve books up there.

We swing by Sadie's house to pick her up. She practically ejects from the front door like a rocket when Ash's car pulls up in front. She runs down the front walk, leaps into the backseat, and says, "Step on it."

Ash, being a good friend, floors it. We blast off from Sadie's quiet little street like Thelma and Louise.

"Problem?" I ask over the roar of the engine.

"Decker didn't want me to leave. He's spent exactly one day with his babies in the last two weeks, and it's—" She makes air quotes. "—too much for him."

"Tough shit," Ash says, tapping on the brakes just lightly enough not to kill us all as we turn the corner. "We have drinks to drink."

"Where are we headed, anyway?" I ask.

"Tai One On," Ash says, accelerating again. "We were supposed to be there at seven. And it's already five after." Ash gets crazy when she's late for anything.

Wait.

"Supposed to?" I ask. "If it's just the three of us, who cares?"

Ash winces.

"Ash?"

"Mmm?" she says, eyes on the road.

"Is it just the three of us?"

"Mmm."

"Ash!" I'm squawking her name as she pulls up to Tai One On, a Tiki place we visit on a semi-occasional basis. "What's happening right now?"

"Mai tais. Duh."

I grab her arm before she can get out of the car. "What are you not telling me?" Her eyes grow wide, and I just *know*. "He's in there, isn't he? My gardener is in there."

She gives me a tiny nod.

"OMIGOD!" I shriek. "No. Nope. No. Uh-uh."

"But I already said we'd—"

"Ash! You tricked me! You tricked your oldest friend. That's mean!"

"Yes," she says with a sigh. "I did, sweetie."

"You always do things like this!"

"I do," she agrees.

"You always have to be in control of every situation!"

"I know. It's a sickness."

"STOP AGREEING WITH ME!" I scream.

"Okay."

I lunge, but Sadie reaches between us and catches my hands. "Take a deep breath."

"But..."

"*Ash*," Sadie orders. "Apologize for bringing Brynn here under false pretenses."

"I'm sorry," Ash says immediately. "I should have told you he was coming. But you need to go in there."

"Not happening!" I argue, shaking off Sadie's grasp.

"You're going to sit down with him and—"

"No. Nooooo!"

"—lick his testicles."

That stops me.

I mean, that's just not something someone says out loud.

Sadie snorts.

"I am not...licking...his...God!" I sorta like this idea. I've eaten cow testicles and they're pretty tasty.

But I digress.

My face is burning. Maybe it is actually on fire, and I am three seconds away from ending up in the *Guinness Book of World Records* as the sorry single woman who spontaneously combusted outside a tiki bar. Not cool.

"Brynn, goddamn it!" Ash really does sound sort of pissed at me.

Although, it could be low blood sugar. We've been shopping for hours, and they have great appetizers here. I can almost hear the pupu platter calling my name.

"He wants to see you. Braht said he's *pining* over you. Pining! Do you know how rare that is? Sadie! Tell her!"

Sadie nods. "As rare as having a third nipple."

"See?" Ash says. "Fuck. I want to be pined over. But nooooo! All I can seem to get is fucking Braht trying to stick his tongue in my ear."

"Are you sure it's his tongue?" Sadie asks.

"Ewwwww!" Ash and I say. But it's also really funny, and we all laugh for a minute.

Then I cross my arms over my new, improved chest, still unwilling to be conned. But secretly (secretly!) I've been pining too. Maybe. Or maybe it was closer to obsessing, but I've really been trying not to be creepy. "I thought you told me that if I was attracted to a guy it was a red flag and I should stay away."

"I did say that," Sadie admits. "But this is not someone you would normally be attracted to. This is the exception that proves the rule."

Damn it. "I don't know," I hedge. "You told me to fuck someone, and I did. But if I walk in there right now, that's *dating*. That wasn't part of the plan."

Ash looks at me like I have something weird sprouting from my forehead. "Are you *blind?* This sort of man doesn't come around very often. Did you see his muscles? Did you not say that was the most amazing moment of your life? Did you not make Sadie and I mad with jealousy?"

"I was a little jealous," Sadie admitted. "The only sexual adventures Decker and I have had is we once had sex in the spare bedroom. On top of the duvet." There's a pause here because what do you say to that? I'm sorry?

"Okay. Right. So. Maybe it's just...just...just..." I really can't finish that sentence. I'm not actively trying to be annoying. But I'm feeling cornered. I try to wiggle the truth free. "I just don't know if I'm ready."

It's the closest to the truth I can get. I really don't know if I'll ever be ready. I don't know if I'm ready to put myself out there again and risk not being attractive enough, or funny enough, or hot enough, or just plain *enough* enough.

I wasn't enough for Steven. Why would I be enough for a man like Tom? A man so manly that he probably flosses with beaver fur. Then I sort of laugh because I just thought of a beaver and beavers always make me laugh. Beeeeaaaver. Furry beavers. *Snort!*

To cover up the snort, I quickly say, "Okay."

"Okay?" Ash asks.

"Fine! Okay, okay? I'll go. But you guys are going too, right?"

Ash and Sadie look at each other. "Of course we are," Ash says slowly.

"Are you guys pulling another fast one on me?"

"No," Sadie says slowly. "We'll go too. It won't be awkward at all, having us along on your date. With your hot gardener."

"Did I ever tell you about his man-hands?" I ask.

"His man hands?" Sadie asks.

"They were a little dirty. He had dirty Man Hands." I don't know why I'm saying this out loud. "They were big and rough. Callused. Like, I don't know, like he actually worked for a living. Like he sweat for a living. They were masculine hands. And he'd just been digging in the dirt so he smelled a little earthy. Dirty-man earthy. He moved them over me and it was like he could hold all of me and still handle more." I realize I'm in the midst of a monologue and Ash and Sadie are just staring at me.

"Man Hands," Ash whispers.

"Filthy, dirty Man Hands," Sadie says.

I nod because, frankly, I'm too turned on to speak.

"I want to get me some of those," Ash says. I think Sadie just gulps.

13 WELCOME ABOARD THE TITANIC

Tom

Hypothetically, let's just say you're on the Titanic. You've helped all the women and children onto lifeboats because that's the kind of guy you are. Those boats are sailing away into the cold night. You're left on the ship, and it's going down. What kind of friend would you want with you at this moment?

I'll tell you one thing. It sure as fuck isn't Braht.

For one, he talks too much. Two, he'd have finagled his way onto one of those lifeboats and stolen your identity. Three, because...

Fuck this long metaphor.

Three, because when the woman you fucked in the boathouse shows up at the tiki bar, your friend and hers make a hasty exit, leaving you alone to sink slowly down to the bottom of the ocean.

Here's how it goes down. At seven on the dot, Braht and I show up. Then three women appear: Ash, the realtor who Braht can't stop eye-fucking, Sadie, a soft and poet-looking woman, and...holy shit... Brynn. Brynn the great. The round. The beautiful. Brynn in another wrap dress that I know I can have her out of with one simple tug of that little bow on her side.

They show up. We fumble through introductions, then Braht, that fucker, takes Ash and Sadie by the elbow and they all just leave. They waltz off without even ordering a drink or offering an explanation. And I'm standing there, and Brynn is standing there, and I don't know if I'm supposed to kiss her or hug her or do a head nod and 'sup.

Titanic. Me on board. Sinking.

Fucking Braht.

We eye each other nervously for a moment, and then she extends a fist. I look at her in confusion.

"Let's just pound this out," she says with this awkward grin. Fuck, do I ever want to pound. Then I realize what she's talking about. I tap my fist to hers. Then we both laugh. We laugh because it's so uncomfortable that the only options are to laugh or take off running, and I'm not going to bail on her.

Unfortunately, I can't really speak in sentences. I was inside this woman last week. Just standing beside her is making me crazy. I want to be inside her again, this second. But people would stare.

"Now," I say, and my face immediately turns red. If my producer could see me right now, he'd rip up my contract. I'm paid seven figures to be smooth on TV, and yet I just said "now" for no apparent reason. "Um," I try again. "Let's sit and order some drinks. I could use one. Could you?"

I think I covered that up real nice. Real, real smooth.

We sit. She looks around at the bamboo flooring, the bamboo walls, the fake palms on the ceiling. The twinkle lights. There's a mural of the ocean, and it's so dark in here it feels like the middle of the night. I swear they have fans that blow around tropical flower smells. Or maybe that's just the scent of her hair.

"Did Braht pick the place?" she asks. "He has a thing for tiki stuff."

"He hates it," I say.

"But his party? Didn't he have that Beachbum guy there?"

"Ah. Beachbum Berry. Yeah. I flew him in. I'm sort of... I'm sort of obsessed with tiki culture. I've been all over the world and—" I stop because she looks kind of green. "Are you okay?"

"Wait," she says. "Wait! You hired Beachbum Berry? That was your party? That was *your* house?"

I laugh. "Well, I wouldn't fuck you in just anybody's boathouse. I bought the house last fall and did some renovations. I've got a lot of work to do on the basement—"

I stop again because her green hue is turning red. Merry Christmas! Is she breathing? I push a glass of water her way. She drinks.

"I...uh...you?" She can't seem to speak. Maybe it's a stroke. What the fuck is the thing you're supposed to do when someone's having a stroke? No, I'm just overreacting. I do that lately. It's why I've taken a break from women, and my show.

Luckily, the waitress comes over to save us from this conversation. She's wearing a Hawaiian dress and there's a flower in her hair that looks exactly like a labia with its clitoris all glistening. "Two mai tais." I stammer, eyes down. What did I tell you? Me. Titanic. Going down. That fucker, Braht. It's all his fault.

Brynn's hand is on her chest. Touching the tops of her rounded breasts—her authentic, not-enhanced, rounded breasts that I just want to lay my head on and watch the clouds go by. "I am so sorry!" she says. "I thought you were a gardener. But if you're a gardener, you're doing very well for yourself. That house is enormous!"

That puffs me up a little, I admit. I mean, tell any man he's enormous at *anything* and there will be puffing. Followed by swelling in his briefs. "But I *am* a gardener," I say. She still looks confused. "I'm a master gardener. An electrician. A contractor. I like to do stuff with my hands. I also have a show on H&G Network. *Mr. Fixit Quick?* Ever heard of that?"

She blinks. "Um, no? I'm sorry. I only watch cooking shows."

"Oh." I can't believe I dropped the don't-you-know-who-I-am card, and she really didn't know.

Ocean floor, here I come!

"You have a show...on television?" she asks. There is an adorable furrow between her eyebrows, and I sort of want to lick it.

"Yup. On TV. The boob tube." I'm rambling. Badly.

She smiles. "But you look so normal. Wait—is that offensive?"

I smile back because her smile is gorgeous and she just complimented me. Sort of. "I don't feel very normal most days." Okay, not smooth. "I mean, TV is not the most relaxing industry, but I like the fast pace. Usually."

"What's your last name, Tom?" she asks, pulling out her phone.

"Spanner."

"Huh. And here I thought you'd be something like... Hammmmerrr...smith."

"Uhm. No. Although that does have a ring to it."

"I'm going to Google you."

"No!" I bark, and she practically drops her phone. "Sorry. What if you didn't? I mean, there's just a bunch of people yapping on the internet. You should make up your own mind."

Her eyes widen. "You mean you have fans?"

"Well, sure. A few." I have millions. But only a dick says so. And I do not want her to sit across from me at this table and read my Wikipedia entry. Before last winter, I wouldn't have had any problem with it. Before The Incident, I liked all the female fans' attention.

Not anymore.

"Okay," she says slowly, dropping her phone into her purse. "Then you can't look me up, either. Deal?"

"That's fair," I agree. "Only now I'm desperate to know what you don't want me to see."

She grins. "The selfie cam on Ash's phone hates me. Every shot is like this." She grabs her face and squeezes, distorting her cheeks. "I looth like a Hobbit," she explains through a puckered face, and then we both laugh.

"I think you're beautiful. Obviously."

Her eyes widen. "Really?"

"Really."

She narrows her eyes. "I'm not sure I believe that from a guy who works in television."

"It's not *The Bachelor*, Brynn. I renovate things."

"With tools?" She looks a little dreamy.

"Yeah." Is there another way to renovate things? "Sometimes I just use my hands. Break things apart. Put them back together."

"Oh, wow."

We've been talking about me for a few minutes now, and that's just rude. "What do you do?" I ask.

She pales.

14 ARM WRESTLING CHAMPION

Brynn

The words sort of hang over the table in a speech bubble. *What do you do?*

I try on a few different responses in my mind. *I'm unemployed*, is the most accurate. But so unsexy. *I'm a fireman.* Fun, but a total lie. I don't even know where I got that idea. Thanks, subconscious.

When Tom was Braht's gardener, this was all so much less confusing.

"Well... It's complicated."

He smiles at me, and his eyes lower a little, and I realize that this man, this god, this TV personality is ogling me. That's right. He's *ogling* me. Well, he's actually ogling my girls, but I'll take it. I am not a woman who's been ogled in a really long time, and it feels good. I sort of relax a little bit.

"How is it complicated?" he asks, his eyes holding mine this time.

"Well, I'm not working in my field at the moment."

"What's your field?"

"English language and writing. I taught at a private college. I have a PhD in English. But I just got laid off from my job." I say *laid off* because that sounds way better than fired.

He sits back in his chair a couple of inches. "You're an academic?" He licks his lips.

Goddamn it. I want to lick those lips. I want his lips to lick my lips. Both sets!

Great. Now I'm throbbing.

"I *would* be an academic, if I had a job," I say, clearing my throat. "We can't all have a glam TV job. Sorry. I'm not very exciting. Or tall."

He leans forward slowly, and I have to lean in too. Then he whispers, "You are plenty tall. You wrapped your legs around me just fine."

And then I faint. I go stiff as a board and fall right over.

Okay. Not actually. But internally, I'm a goner.

I take a dainty sip of my drink. Unfortunately, it's empty so it makes a slurpy noise, and because I've already started slurping, I just keep on slurping so I look like I did it all on purpose. Because I'm smooth like that. Silky. Also, I'm an idiot. I can't smile and be sexy and fake it 'til we make it. I can't carry on the charade. Now that we both have our clothes on, he's going to see me as the divorced, jobless loser that I am.

"So, what do you do outside of your field?" He reaches for me with one big Man Hand and tilts my chin so I'm looking at him. The move is very BBC Miniseries. For a second I'm trapped in his chocolatey gaze and everything is okay.

Except he's waiting for an answer. And, goddamn it. How do I tell him I've been too depressed to look for a real job so I mostly sit around the house, make dips and balls and logs and post it on my—

"Blog!" I say. Actually, I sort of shout it. What a stupid word. Blog. Blogblogblog. "I blog!" Why? Why am I shouting? It's like I suddenly have Tourette's. And you shouldn't joke about Tourette's.

"You make a living at that?" He means blogging. Not Tourette's. He sounds either impressed or confused. Maybe both.

"I didn't at first. But now it's starting to take off. It helps my bottom line. I have a little nest egg from..." That word I can barely say. "My *divorce*. I'm working hard on the blog while I send out résumés to English departments." I should send out those résumés, anyway. But I've been waiting for my self-esteem to get up off the floor. "I try out recipes, write about food, take pictures. I've got three cookbooks now. I'm working on the fourth. I can do it from home, and I have an excuse to eat bacon. Not like I need an excuse, because, hello, bacon."

He laughs. It's a real laugh. It's warm and rich.

When he smiles at me, I forget for a second that he's out of my league. When he looks at me that way, I could almost become the fun, confident person he must think I am. "You want to arm wrestle?" I ask. Or maybe it's the empty mai tai that's asked.

He shrugs. "Okay." He leans forward and puts his elbow on the table. I lean forward after settling my boobs on the edge of the table (they're heavy, okay?) and wrap my hand around his. He has the manliest hands I've ever come into contact with, and I instantly have an orgasm. It's a small one, so I'm able to keep it together. Then we lock eyes and everything in the room quiets. "On three," he says. "One—"

I slam his hand down.

See? I can play dirty.

I smile. He smiles. And then Steven walks in the door.

Fucking. A. Steven.

Why do I even care? Why do I care that he strolls in all happy and puffed up like a strutting peacock with that...that girl on his arm. Why do I care? He doesn't have my heart anymore. Or my vows. He doesn't even have access to my bank account. We're as over as over can be.

And that's what it is. That's the thing that's getting me. Six months ago, we shared the same life. I knew where he was every minute of the day, could tell you what he'd wear one day to the next. I could tell by the way he said hello to me if he wanted to have sex. Answer: never. We shared the same life! And now he's a stranger.

Those tears again.

"Hey," Tom says, softly. Then again, "Hey." I realize we're still holding hands.

"That's my ex." I say and do a jerky little head-nod thing. "I don't love him anymore. I don't even care that he's here. It's just..." I don't finish the sentence because I don't know what to finish the sentence with. All of a sudden, I don't need to because Tom has leaned across the table and he kisses me. It's lovely and soft and awkward, so he breaks the kiss, stands up, walks over to me, pulls me up and then kisses me properly.

I don't know if it's for my benefit or because he can tell Steven is watching us, but suddenly I don't care anymore.

I may have been invisible to my ex, but this man, this man right here, he sees me.

When he pulls away, I'm smiling. For a few reasons. 1) The throbbing. 2) Because now he's ordering appetizers. And 3) When I look at Steve to sort of flaunt my hotness and my hot man kissing me, I realize it wasn't Steve at all, but some stranger.

Huh.

15 NAKED SKYDIVING

Tom

I don't know how long we've been here, but it's long enough that I'm drunk. Not on alcohol, actually. I'm drunk with desire. My dick is as hard as rebar, and every few minutes he makes a noise of complaint, and I have to adjust myself just to shut him up.

"So then," I say, and for a second I forget what I was talking about. We are surrounded by empty platters of appetizers: sticky buns, pupu platters, crispy wonton strips. Everything sounds sexual to me. It just does. "I'm sorry," I admit. "I have no idea what I was saying."

"You were saying something about why you're currently *unemployed*." The way Brynn says the word, it's like I should get a ribbon or something. Like she's comforted by that.

"Technically, I'm on hiatus," I say, and then I giggle. Me. A thirty-eight-year-old man. I giggle. Because suddenly, hiatus sounds a lot like high-anus. I don't really find that sexual. "We're on high-anus," I say. I said it. I did. Out loud.

She snorts. "Why? Did you get bored of traveling the world? Meeting exotic women? Playing Mr. Fixit in too many locales?"

She's laughing, and I want to snuggle my manness into her femaleness. But I'm serious. I'm so serious that I'm nodding. "I'm serious. That is exactly what happened. I mean, I've been doing this show for nine seasons now and it's always the same, you know? Go into some house, tear shit down, pound it back up, flirt a little, do too much cocaine, sky dive naked, inject..." Her mouth is open. Wide. I laugh. "I was just seeing if you were paying attention."

"I'm loopy," she says. "But I can still pay attention. Please tell me that last part isn't true." She looks at me with this kind of plea in her eyes, and I want to scoop her into my arms and make everything better. Like, everything. The world. Politics. Cable television. I want to heal everything.

"I don't do drugs. Strictly against it. But I do like to be naked."

"While sky diving?"

"Well, no. There'd be too much...flapping. And you sort of need a parachute for, you know, your life and all. But in my own home, I'm naked a lot."

"You just walk around naked?" she asks. She seems genuinely interested.

I nod. "Sometimes." I lean in and whisper, "I don't even walk around. Sometimes I just sit there."

"And do what? Oh, god! Don't answer that!"

"I just sit on my couch and watch Netflix. There's some quality programming there."

She laughs, and I laugh too. And yes, it's because we're both "loopy" and full of Chinese takeout-type food, and the lighting is dark and moody, and I'm comfortable and horny, yes, all of that, but there's something else. There's an easiness about her that feels just... like she doesn't need fixing at all.

"Come home with me," I say, all conversation about work abandoned. We can get into that later. But for right now, I'm serious. For real. I want her to come home with me. "Spend the night."

"With you? Naked?" She draws out the word a little, like she's weighing the idea.

I'm way past weighing, though. The only thing I want is to be home, in a real bed, with this woman. "Exactly. Let's go get very, very naked."

Her eyes darken, and she takes a quick breath. Then she lets out a little whimper.

We are definitely getting some tonight, my dick says.

Hush, I warn him. Silently this time.

"I can't," she says, sitting back in her chair.

Wait, really?

"Wait, really?" I say aloud. "Is there someone else?" This idea panics me, and not just because I don't like cheaters. I'm so wound up right now that the idea of someone else putting his mitts on Brynn makes me feel a little insane.

Slowly, she shakes her head. "I can't, because we'll ruin it."

"Ruin what?"

"The boathouse," she whispers. "It was *perfect*."

I run this statement through my brain a few times, trying to figure out what's wrong. I've never been super smart, but this just doesn't make sense. "It was perfect," I agree. "You don't think I can bring the magic again? Hell. I'm just warming up."

Her eyes flare. But then she shakes it off. "I really can't take that risk. You of all people should understand, since you know Hollywood."

"What?" My show is produced out of New York. But it's rude to correct a lady, and it's just stupid to argue with someone you're trying to get naked.

"Think of all the bad remakes!" she says, her pretty face suddenly horrified. "Remakes always flop. Everyone knows this. Hello, *Psycho*?" She shakes her head again at the travesty. "And *The Bad News Bears*."

"Hmm." I see her point. "*Point Break*, too. And *Dirty Dancing*."

She swallows hard. "You've watched the original *Dirty Dancing*?"

Whoops. I have to make a quick calculation—truth or lie? Seems like a bad idea to lie to the girl you're crushing on. "Yeah. I've watched it way more than once. It's like an old friend I used to know. Sometimes it's lonely when we're shooting in a town I don't know. Rewatching movies is nice."

She puts a hand to her bosom and sighs happily, and I smile at her because it's such a pretty sight.

"Do I lose my man card for that?"

"No sir. The world has changed. You can keep your man card. Actually, you get a gold star on it for liking *Dirty Dancing*."

"Good." I place my elbows on the table and lean closer. If those kisses I got earlier are all I can have tonight, I'll take it. It's probably madness for a guy who works with his hands to argue with a PhD, but

I'm thinking I need to give it the old I-didn't-make-it-through-college try. "Listen. I don't want a remake."

"What?" Her expression dims.

"You're right. Remakes are terrible. But that was never the plan."

"It wasn't?"

I shake my head. "This was meant to be a series, not a one-time blockbuster. Our night in the boathouse was just the...pilot episode."

She blinks, and I have the sudden urge to kiss her eyelashes.

I've got it bad.

"Now, most people would put episode two in my king-sized bed. That's the obvious script. We could tie your wrists to the headboard, and I could put your ankles on my shoulders and bang you into next Tuesday."

Brynn gulps.

"...but if you want the season to be a true success, we should really save that until later on. So episode two should be the kitchen counter. We could go back to my place and make something for dessert. Like, I dunno..."

"Cherry pie," she breathes. Her cheeks are stained pink, and her pupils are blown.

"Right! You're good at this. Cherry pie. There will be flour and stuff all over the countertops when we're done, right?"

She nods slowly, her eyes never leaving mine. And she licks her lips a little.

"Right. So. The pie is baking in the oven, but that takes a while. While we're waiting for it, I kiss you. And things get a little heated, so I have to sweep the rolling pin right off the counter top—" I mime swiping everything off our table. "—and hoist you up and just do you right there while the pie bakes."

Her chest is heaving, and both her hands have a white-knuckled grip on the table. She's definitely buying what I'm selling.

And since I've hit my stride—because planning killer TV shows is my calling—I just keep going. "Episode three is a shower scene. Duh. But I have this rather rough stone in my shower, and I don't want to bruise your spine against the surface. Ouch, right? So I'll just have to pick you up and bounce you on my dick."

Yesss! my dick shouts.

"Hang on pal," I tell him. I'm pretty sure I don't say that out loud, but whatever. I'm on a roll here. "Episode four could be the bed, I suppose. But a lounge chair on the patio sounds even better. No—the hot tub! Or a bubble bath. I want to wipe soap bubbles all over your tits…"

Holy shit. I'm *aching* now. My dick feels like reinforced concrete. I'll have to invest in roomier shorts if I'm going to woo Brynn with dirty talk. And is it hot in here?

My girl isn't faring much better. She looks like she might burst into flames across the table. So it's time to put us both out of our misery. "A series, Brynn. Not a remake. Let's go back to my place and do some…" I drop my voice low. "Storyboarding."

Wordlessly, she grabs her handbag off the back of the chair and stands up.

I rise, rifling through my wallet. I leave a stack of bills. My truck is out in back, and Brynn's friends dropped her off, so we don't even have to argue about who's driving.

She leans into my chest when I put my arm around her as we walk toward the door. The warmth of her body against mine is crazy-making. I want this woman with every ounce of my being. Since I'm six-three and two hundred fifteen pounds, that's a lot of ounces.

I guide her to the door. We open it and step outside.

Then the world explodes into light.

16 GIANT MAN TRUCK

Brynn

It takes a while for my lust-addled brain to make sense of the blinding lights washing over me. They're flashbulbs. Lots of them.

"Look over here, Tom!" a voice shouts.

"Who's the lucky girl?" another yells.

"What the..." Beside me, Tom is flustered too. But he shakes it off faster than I do. "Brynn, honey, this way." One of his brawny arms steers me around the side of the building. "The red truck," he says tersely. "Go!"

Apparently I'm good at taking directions. For the second time in a week I take off running just because someone urged me to. I break for the truck, and its taillights flash as I approach, signaling that it's unlocked.

"Hey, Brynn!" a voice shouts from the mob behind us. "What's your last name, little bunny?"

"Don't answer that," Tom barks. He's right behind me. The way Tom is parked, it's the driver's side of the truck that's facing us. Tom catches my hand in one of his, then yanks the driver's side door open.

It's sort of amazing that he's able to whisk me right off the ground and onto the seat. I've never been whisked before, and it's nice. It really is. Then he pats my hip and I like it so much that for a moment it escapes me that he wants me to scoot over.

I scoot, sliding across the macho leather seats of Tom's giant Man Truck.

He's seated beside me and cranking the engine not a second later. The locks click down with a thunk, and he throws on the headlights. A pack of paparazzi shield their eyes from the glare. He revs the engine, and they scatter. It's sort of a Keystone Cop kind of thing, all this scattering, and even though things are a little intense right now, I laugh. Because that's what I do with intensity. Laugh right in its face. Take that, inten— And we're moving. I forgot we were having a moment, but Tom saying, "That's right, assholes. *Move*," reminds me.

The truck heaves forward. The tires screech, and a moment later we've left them all behind in the dust. I hear a couple of them coughing, even.

We drive.

Or rather Tom drives, and I sort of breathe heavily. I have to admit, his alpha-ness just then was sorta hot. In English departments, there aren't paparazzi or big trucks, and I think that's really a shame. "Wow," I say, and I mean it.

"I know," Tom says, "I'm making excellent time." Leave it to a man to be conscious of making good time. Though he is hitting all the lights just right. I'm still kind of woozy from remembering him list all the rooms of his house where boinking should happen. Would happen. Would be happening imminently. But as my lust dials back from eleven to, say, a nine, I realize that he looks tense. "Okay, is that whole scene...normal for you?"

"No, not at all. Not since..." He cringes.

"Since when? I didn't even know they had paparazzi in Michigan. I thought they maybe shriveled up in the cold."

"I thought that too," he says through gritted teeth. "That's why I've been hiding here."

"*Hiding?*" Oh god, maybe Tom is some kind of psycho serial killer. "Hiding from the cops?"

"No! Did they look like cops to you?"

Maybe. The kind in silent movies. But I don't say that out loud. Sometimes my imagination runs away with me. A tiny bit. Just enough to make life interesting. "Why are all those people with cameras chasing you?"

He glances into the rearview mirror. "I have no idea, but it can't be good." He reaches for his phone in the cup holder and hands it to me. "Can you look at my texts? My agent's name is Patricia. Whatever's going on, she'd be the one to know."

I take the phone, and indeed, there is a string of texts lighting up the security screen and I don't suppose that psycho serial killers are willing to hand off their phones. This is somewhat comforting to me.

"The passcode is H-O-M-E," he says.

I tap that in. "Your first message is from Braht. It says: **What color are her panties this time?**" Ugh. "You told him about my Easter panties?"

"They were the only clue I had! Next time, leave behind your business card."

The man makes a good point. "Your next message is from Patricia. She says: **That's one way to tell the world that you're back on the market**."

"I have no idea what that means." Tom shakes his head.

My own phone is dancing a jig in my handbag. So I pull it out.

> *Ash: Oh, honey. We're here for you.*
> *Sadie: Wow. You weren't kidding. I'm sorry the*
>   *world is seeing that, but it really WAS the*
>   *hottest sex ever to hit a boathouse. *Fans self**
> *Ash: Sadie, she doesn't want to hear that*
>   *right now.*
> *Sadie: Why not. If I just broke the internet with*
>   *my sex tape, I'd want to know it was a good one.*

"OH MY GOD!" I shriek. "THAT'S WHY THE PHOTOGRAPHER CALLED ME LITTLE BUNNY!" I really do say that in all caps because what's happening in my brain is in all caps and it includes my Easter panties, his giant cock, and me revving like a lawn mower.

"What's the matter?" Tom is maneuvering his giant Man Truck between the gates of his mansion. But instead of waiting for an answer, he slams the truck into park and jumps out.

As I spin around in my seat to watch, he slams the gates closed, wraps a thick metal chain around the joining parts, then padlocks them together.

Another set of headlights appears beyond the gates. "Fuck," Tom says. He gives the car the finger and then does a flying leap back into the truck. He really has some superhero moves, this Tom.

If I weren't freaking out right now, I'd probably find it hot.

He parks the truck inside his giant four-stall garage and then kills the engine. Everything goes dark, including my phone because I've stuffed it back into my bag, hoping against all hope that I've leapt to the wrong conclusion. We sit there a moment in the silence while my brain explodes.

"Can you tell me what's the matter?" he asks, his voice deep and smoky beside me.

"S-something about a sex t-tape," I stammer. It can't be true. It just can't.

"A...what?" He grabs his phone off the seat and starts scrolling. His frown is illuminated by the blue light. And he's handsome even like that, damn it.

My thoughts are like a popcorn machine without the top on. Bouncing all over the place.

And now I'm a little hungry for popcorn. I like it really salty and with so much butter that your hand glistens with popcorn magic and — FOCUS BRYNN!

"Holy shit," Tom whispers. "Jesus H." He stabs the screen one more time, and then there's a soundtrack. First, a female sigh and a moan. The indistinct growl of a sexy man.

My traitorous nipples harden immediately. Down, girls!

"Unnnh," the female voice says. "Fuck me. FUCK ME."

Every inch of my skin goes cold the moment I recognize my own voice. But even then I'm not absolutely sure. This couldn't be happening to me. Holding my breath, I lean over to see Tom's screen.

Now, when you get really stressed out, your brain makes some weird accommodations. For five seconds or so my mind refuses to acknowledge the right half of the video on Tom's phone. And the left half is glorious! There is a fine pair of muscular man buns clenching on each erotic thrust. I could watch that all day.

But then my subconscious dares me to take in the rest of the frame. And I look.

And I really shouldn't have.

"Omigod," I gasp. "Oh. God. Tell me that's not on the internet. Where did you get that? DID YOU TAKE THAT VIDEO OF ME? Omigod."

Tom stops the video and drops the phone like a hot potato. "Brynn, I'm so fucking sorry."

"Did you do this?"

"No! I'd *never*... God, no! I don't know who took that. Only a monster would do that. Well, only a monster would *share* it, because, actually, that was some seriously fine footage—"

A slap rings out, and I think it was from me. I've smacked his big biceps in anger.

Tom grabs my hands and holds them together. Then he dips his head and kisses my palms quickly. "Brynn, listen. We'll get to the bottom of this. I'll fix it. I promise you."

"You can't *fix* it," I sob. "They've already seen! When it's seen, it cannot be unseen! It's burned into all their retinas!"

"Who are 'they,' exactly? And retinas burn? Really?"

I'm a little hysterical now. Though he's right—it's unclear who's seen what, and maybe I'm panicking for nothing. But once you see someone fucking, it's hard to picture them doing their taxes. They're always fucking! Even at a funeral. If my friends already know about this video—and a horde of photographers know—it must be serious.

"I'll do whatever it takes, honey. Calm down."

"I WILL NOT CALM DOWN!" I don't even know why he'd tell me to calm down. Oh wait, maybe I do. I'm shouting and vibrating like a scared Chihuahua.

"Will you come inside with me? I need to call my agent and make sure she gets to the bottom of this."

"O-k-k-kay," I say, as my teeth chatter. "What if my mother sees it?" Actually, I can't worry about that yet. She only watches the Home Shopping Network.

"I know this is bad," he says. "But I need you to come inside with me so I can try to figure it out."

"D-do you have any chocolate?" I whimper. "It's good for shock." I ask for chocolate because I'm pretty sure "making a cherry pie and getting fucked on the counter" is off the table.

"Hmm. I don't have straight-up chocolate, but I do have it in ice cream form," he says.

"Close enough."

I follow him inside.

17 CHOCOLATE MOUSSE

Tom

Brynn is rattled, and it's all my fault.

Okay, it's not *really* my fault. I never filmed her, and I certainly would never share a video of that on the internet. If I'm ever naked with Brynn again, I'll hold her as closely as those crazy people on *Hoarders* cling to their garbage.

But not in a creepy way. I am not a creep! But, hell, why would this woman ever believe me? We had sex once, and now it's all over the internet.

In my kitchen, she's buzzing around like a nervous bee. And— even worse—I'm out of chocolate ice cream. She's flinging cabinets open. I don't mind at all, except that she's stressed.

"Aha!" she yells, grabbing a container of Hershey's unsweetened cocoa.

"I don't even know why I have that," I hedge. My ex must have bought it.

"Stand back!" she says. "I know what I'm doing." She tugs the top off and takes a deep, worshipful sniff of the contents.

"Okay..." I walk slowly backward, leaving her in the kitchen. By the time I'm out of the room she's grabbed a carton of eggs from the refrigerator and a carton of heavy cream.

I leave her to it.

Thirty seconds later I'm on the phone with my agent, Patricia. My agent is one hundred percent Don't Fuck With Me New Yorker, accent and all. "We found the source," she says without any preamble. Good ol' New Yorker. No time for bullshit. "Someone sold it to *Like a Hawk*."

"What the fuck is that?"

"A skeezy blog. They paid five grand for it."

"I'll pay six to get it back."

"You already offered ten," she says. "They'll take it. They already had their fun. But it's been downloaded thousands of times already."

"Fuck!"

"Yes, that's a good title for it. Nice work, hot buns. Who hates you, anyway?"

I growl into the phone. But she asks a good question. "Could have been anyone. My college buddy threw the party at my place just because he likes that patio."

"So you don't know who to sue?"

"Nope. We'll have to do this your way. But if it's been downloaded all over hell, why
buy it back?"

"When you own the video, you can file takedown notices under the Digital Millennium Copyright Act. Thirteen states don't have laws against nonconsensual porn, so this is your best option."

"So they can just violate my girl's privacy and it's not even against the law?" I hate the whole world and everyone in it. I hate parallel universes too. That's how angry I am.

"Look on the bright side, Tom. This is going to be killer for your ratings. I'll bet the network is raising the prices on your summer rerun advertising as we speak!"

My growl is so loud the neighbors probably suspect a bear.

"Now, now. Chin up. Step back and let me do my job, hon."

That's twice in two minutes that women have asked me to step back. And both of them had their reasons. "Okay," I say, weariness in my voice. "What else?"

"Emergency PR meeting tomorrow, first thing. We have to figure out how you want to spin this."

"Spin it? I want it gone."

"And I want a blue pony and a personal sex god named Sven! Conference call at nine. Be there, big guy."

She hangs up, and I just stand there with my phone pressed against my head for another couple of minutes. I'm trying to get the image out of my mind of Patricia riding Sven like a blue pony, and it's a really hard image to shake off. I'm also seething mad. I need a minute to focus. To breathe. To recalibrate. So I contemplate my big, empty living room. I hate this house. I really do. I renovated it during season nine for a woman who did not want me. And now every day I wander around these rooms, looking at her decor choices, wondering how I could have been so dumb.

I have to do a whole lot of deep breathing before I go back into the kitchen to check on Brynn. She's using a big KitchenAid mixer that I am positive has never even been plugged in before. It's here because of the color—green apple—which looks smashing against the glass tiles.

"Hi," I shout over the noise. "Everything okay?"

It's totally not, though, and I already know this.

"It will be!" Brynn shouts back. "In about one and a half minutes."

There's something white and fluffy in the bowl, but I don't care what it is. I'm too busy being baffled by the sight of the pretty lady in my kitchen. Her spine is straight and her sweet face is calm. She's operating the giant mixer with the orderly grace of a NASA commander preparing a rocket launch.

No woman has ever cooked anything in my kitchen before this moment. And I don't mean just *this* kitchen. Any kitchen.

I take a seat on a stool (paint color: distressed nickel) and just watch.

The view soothes me. Brynn takes a small saucepan of what looks like chocolate syrup off the stove and stirs it lovingly. I don't recognize any of the utensils or even the pan, even though they're mine. I don't really cook.

My ex didn't, either, now that I think about it. And yet I'd bought all these things feeling absolutely certain that I could create a happy life on this property with a little wishful thinking and my Amex black card.

Brynn pours the chocolatey stuff into the white fluffy stuff. Then she uses a paddle-shaped thing to combine them. She's sort of lifting the fluff over the chocolate in slow, certain strokes.

I'm getting a little turned on, my dick whispers.

Huh. I'd actually forgotten about him for a while.

"What is that you're making?" I ask quietly, hoping she won't remember that I've probably ruined her peace for the foreseeable future.

"Chocolate mousse. Do you have parfait cups?"

"What are those?"

Without a glance in my direction she turns around and begins opening and shutting cabinets again. It's a huge kitchen, so this takes a while. "Aha!" she finally says, grabbing two glass dishes that look like extra-sturdy wine glasses. She tips the bowl and sort of encourages the mousse to fill first one cup and then the other. She opens the fridge again and puts the cups inside.

And then? She licks the paddle. Her tongue comes out and sweeps the chocolate off one edge. Slowly.

Ungh, my dick says. *What about my needs?*

Seriously.

Her gaze lifts to mine. "Want a lick?"

"Do I ever," I rumble. Then I realize she means the chocolate.

But, hey, when I get a taste, that's pretty good too. "Wow. You're amazing."

For a split second her face lights up. Then it shuts down again.

"What did I say?"

"Men always love the cooking." She sighs. "Anyway. I feel a little calmer now. Sometimes when I'm really emotional, I cook something and things go back to being balanced. I don't know why. So. What did your agent say?"

"She's working on buying the video back. I'll know a lot more tomorrow."

"Okay," she whispers. "I'm trying not to panic prematurely."

I rise from the stool and walk around the counter. Then I pull her to my chest. "You're a trooper, Brynn. I'm going to do my best to clear up this mess as fast as I can."

"I know," she says, sighing against me. Her hair smells like flowers. I want to do that thing I described where I sweep everything off the counter and ravage her. But there are a few little blobs of chocolate goo there now. So if I did, it would ruin her dress.

Even worse, I don't think you can ravage someone whose privacy your fans have just invaded. So I give her a tight hug instead.

"LtsrtChocMss," she says against my shirt.

"Hmm?" I lean back so she can breathe and she looks up at me with her wide eyes.

"Let's eat chocolate mousse."

"Okay."

The chocolate mousse is almost as good as an orgasm.

Not true, my dick argues. But I ignore him.

Meanwhile, Brynn's friends are worried about her. They keep texting. "Can you take me home?" she asks with big, scared eyes. "I need to regroup."

"Of course," I say, wishing she'd just come upstairs to bed with me. "There are, uh, photographers at the gate, though."

"You don't think they gave up?" She actually looks scared.

"Most of them probably did. But there's always one asshole who hides in the bushes all night."

Her eyes narrow. "I thought you said this didn't usually happen to you."

"It doesn't." Except for last spring, of course. *Ugh.* "I have a plan, though. Can you text your friends and ask them to pick you up at Rosie's Boat Launch across the lake? I can get you there in private."

"Yeah?" She looks so relieved that my heart breaks a little. "Sure. At least it's a plan."

18 KISS DE GIRL

Brynn

After I send my RESCUE ME text to Sadie and Ash, Tom grabs my hand and motions for me to follow him across his shiny marble floors and into the basement. It occurs to me to wonder whether there's some kind of Fifty Shades of Dungeon down there, but thankfully, there's not.

Although I wouldn't mind having Tom as a slave, rubbing my feet. While wearing nothing but a tie. That. Would. Be. Hot.

We whip by some unfinished rooms. This house may be a mansion, but it's all cold. Not just the floors, but the walls and the ceiling and the perfect accessories and the perfectly placed splashes of color. It's like walking quietly through the pages of a magazine. It's a little bit eerie, to tell the truth.

After an hour, and maybe that's an exaggeration, he takes me into this tunnel. I shit you not. And we end up in the boathouse. Yes. *The* Boathouse.

I start to hyperventilate.

"Are you hyperventilating?" he asks.

Fuck.

He digs around and hands me a paper bag. Tom is an absolute boy scout. I control my breathing while remembering that night when we fucked at first sight. It'd be a purely amazing memory if I couldn't now envision the creeper outside the window with their phone. To make sure there isn't an actual creeper there now, I peek out, but we're safe. And while I did all of that, Tom has rattled around a bit and tosses something slightly damp and bulky over my shoulders. Then he starts zipping me up and tying me into it. See? Fifty Shades!

Or a life jacket.

"After the night we've had, I just want to be extra safe," he says. I agree. If ever there was a night when I'd be struck by lightning in a watercraft, it would be tonight.

I look at the sleek wooden boat or yacht or what have you, and my eyes get a little misty.

"Is that—?" I can't finish the sentence. He's going to whisk me away in that? Hell yes! It's all my wildest BBC fantasies come true, but first I need to toss water over him so his shirt is sticking to him and I can see his Man Chest through the wonderfully transparent shirt...

"Ah, no," he whispers. "That." He points. To an actual blow-up dinghy.

And naturally I giggle at the phrase "blow-up dinghy."

"It's not very romantic," he says, "but honestly, I'm a pretty practical guy."

He's practical, gorgeous, and he can lift a dinghy with his bare hands!

I giggle again.

We tiptoe to the beach and he gently slides the dinghy into the water. He offers me his hand and I gingerly step in, then almost fall over because me and coordination do not mix. "Whoa!" he says and steadies me with those Man Hands of his. Then he says, "Shhhhh," and we both go still and quiet, listening for any prowling paparazzi, but there aren't any. Or if they're prowling, they're upstairs peeking into windows. There are a lot of windows at his mansion, so we should be good for a while. I sit down, and he gives the boat a shove and nimbly jumps in.

For a moment we just glide across the water, then he begins to paddle, the oar dipping into the water with a plop. Then there's a slight whoosh of water and the lapping of the waves. The stars twinkle in the sky above us, and any minute I am certain there's going to be a crab popping up and singing to us to kiss.

Too much Disney in my life. No wonder I'm not the practical one in this dinghy.

I sit there quietly, trying to wrap my head around the night's adventures.

I should be feeling all sorts of things right now. And I am, just not the things you'd expect. I should be mad at him for the video and pissed at whoever posted it and terrified that I'm looking for a job while my ass is getting splashed all over the internet.

But what I really feel? Right now in this moment, in the center of the lake, with Tom rowing me to safety? I feel...content. I feel safe.

I never felt safe with Steve. With him, I felt like I was a weight clinging to his legs, trying to pull him under.

I clear my throat because I'm sad again all of a sudden. And this lifejacket is chafing me.

We make it to the other side of the lake without sinking, and really, without saying a word. When we pull up, an SUV flashes its lights twice. There's a pause, and then Ash does that whisper-shout thing of "WE'RE HERE!"

"GOT IT!" I whisper-shout back. Then they flash the lights three more times in case I've had a brain injury in the last ten seconds.

"Okay, then," I say. I'm not sure what to do. We'd had a fun time, he got me all heated, I was traumatized by that video, and now I'm on the beach of Reed's Lake making my quick escape. "See ya," I offer lamely and turn toward Ash, Sadie, and the babies.

"Hey! Wait!" he says, and my heart does a little jump.

I turn to him and wait.

"The lifejacket?"

"Oh."

He reaches for me and unclips the jacket, and it falls off me. It sorta feels like I'm standing here naked now. I guess, symbolically, I am.

"Listen, I'm really sorry about tonight and I promise you...I promise I'll fix this."

I raise my eyebrow in a question. "But can you Fixit Quick?"

He smiles. It's that fuckable smile I've caught a glimpse of a couple of times now, and it makes me throb. In my lady bits.

"Well, that is technically my name. I'll figure out something by tomorrow, okay?"

The horn blares and we jump and Ash, apparently fed up with the incognito spy life shouts, "Oh for fuck's sake, kiss her already!"

He does.

It's soft. Sweet. Slow.

Then he jumps into his dinghy and escapes.

My hero! In his dinghy.

I giggle again because, come on, *dinghy* is just a ridiculous word.

19 TO WHOM IT MAY CONCERN, THOSE ARE MY PANTIES

Brynn

I'm a maelstrom of emotions. Maelstrom. Which is sorta like *male storm*, and isn't that appropriate? So my emotions are swirling in my mind like mad, along with the image of me being fucked by the very masculine, and handy, Tom. I'd be turned on if I weren't mortified. I *am* mortified. I'm mortified and a mess, and this is not the state to be in when I'm trying to write an email seeking a tenure-track position in teaching. Or any track position. No one wants professors anymore, least of all professors who specialize in narrative and expository essays.

And who better to mold young, malleable minds than naked, humping me?

At any rate, I've got to focus and take care of my life, and taking care of my life means pulling up my big-girl panties (they're sporting chicks today, but fuck it) and get that job.

TO WHOM IT MAY CONCERN:

I am seeking a tenure-track position in English Literature and Language.

My specialty is poetry and being fucked by a stranger in a boathouse,

Because that's poetry, man.

Yeah.
Probably not the impression I want to make.
Delete.

TO WHOM IT MAY CONCERN:

I am seeking a tenure-track position, but I'll basically take anything, except an adjunct position, because, come on, you can afford to pay someone a decent wage.

FYI, I was fired from my last teaching job not just because of downsizing, but because the universe fucking hates me. And if you Google my name to see if I'll be a good influence on your students, you'll see how passionate I am about...

TO WHOM IT MAY CONCERN:

Please consider me for an adjunct position. I'm real smart. Smartitude. That's me.

TO WHOM IT MAY CONCERN:

There's no way you're going to hire me. Not in a million years. Not with me spread-eagle and grunting in a boathouse. Not with that close-up of my panties with the bunnies on them. I'm the worst mistake you could ever make, and no student will take me seriously.

By the fifth try, I'm not even crying. I'm too numb.

I have to fix this. I'm going to be unemployed and begging for gruel in two months if I don't fix this quick.

That phrase makes me think of Tom. He'll fix this, right?

I want to believe it. But life experience has taught me that waiting for men is a bad idea. It's like waiting for a sale on wrap dresses, only to find that it's just a ten percent discount on the yellow dresses that clash with my skin.

Too little, too late.

20 YUMMY BALLS

Brynn

Ash and I are camped out at my place. All the curtains are drawn, because the photographers have found me now. There are at least a dozen of them outside my house. They took photos of Ash's butt as she walked up the driveway.

Ash has a nicer than average butt. Even so, I wish the world would just go away.

We're eating popcorn on my sofa, and I'm pouting.

There's a video of me on the internet having sex. It's still there. I know because my mother is having a heart attack every hour. One of her besties from church saw it and called her.

"I need to change my name," I say suddenly, dipping my hand into the popcorn bowl again.

"Because of the job-hunting thing?" Ash asks. She's bathed in the light of my computer screen. I can't bear to look at my inbox, so she's doing it for me.

"The job-hunting thing is pretty crucial," I admit. "It's a shame, because I always liked being Brynn. It's unusual. It rhymes with 'grin.'"

"What are you going to call yourself?"

"No idea yet. Something else the rhymes with grin? Shin? Spin? What are you doing?"

She taps away on my keyboard. "I'm deleting all the dick pics."

"People are sending dick pics? This is why I'm changing my name. I could be...Berlin!"

"No. Your name stays the same. Maybe you could just close your Facebook account. That sounds easier."

"No one will hire me without Googling my name."

Ash flinches, and that's how I know it's really bad. Ash isn't a flincher. Once, in college, she fought off two muggers with one high-heeled shoe. "It will blow over eventually," she says.

"The internet never forgets. I also have to change my face."

"What?"

"My face. I can't keep this one. It's no good."

She looks up. "Not sure you have a choice. Don't go all *Silence of the Lambs* on me."

"Ew! No worries. I don't like fava beans and Chianti."

"I know."

"But—" This is the thing I can't get past. "—the internet has *seen my sex face*. Before last night, that was private. Even *I* hadn't seen my sex face! And I would have liked to keep it that way!"

Ugh.

"I'm sorry, honey," Ash says, patting my hand. "I would switch places with you if I could."

"Really?"

"Sure! It would probably be great for my real estate business." She sits back as a dreamy look steals across her face. "I think I should claim to be a porn star. It doesn't even have to be true. I could triple my listings."

I give her a little kick. "You're mocking me."

"I'm not!" She looks up in alarm. "I'll prove it."

She starts to turn the screen in my direction, but I look away. "Don't show me my sex face!"

"Calm down. We're looking at your blog stats."

"I haven't posted anything new in three days!" My whole life was going to hell, and I didn't even have a carefully styled pastry to eat while Rome burns.

"They don't care, Brynnie. Look."

The graph of my daily unique visitors looks like a cliff in the Alps. A flattish line bumbles along from left to right and then leaps up.

"What the hell? Is this thing broken? I can't have forty thousand unique visitors today."

"Au contraire, mon frère!" Ash cackles. "Scandal is good for web hits. Also, you have a really nice sex face. My sex face looks like I just farted."

"Holy cannoli," I breathe, eyeing the stats, not responding to Ash's sex-fart-face.

"You know what would really make you feel better? You could make us some cannoli. From scratch," Ash suggests. "That sounds really good right about now."

"I'm not your personal chef." Lately it makes me touchy when people ask me to cook for them.

Ash pokes me. "I'm not Steve, damn it. I'm just hungry, and we can't go out for a boozy lunch because there are photographers camped out on the front walk. I'll cook for you if you want me to, but we both know where that will lead us."

She's right. The ER. Ash can cause food poisoning while fixing up nothing but air. She's magic that way.

We do need food, damn it. "I'll see what I can scare up. This popcorn isn't going to last forever." This kind of crisis requires frequent snacking. "Hey—look at my Amazon ranking, would you?" I heave myself off the couch and wander toward the kitchen. I'm not in the mood for sweet things. Stress calls for salty things, and since I can't have sex right now, I'll just make some artichoke dip.

"Hey!" Ash calls out a minute later. "*Yummy Balls* is ranked ninety-seven."

I ponder the interior of my refrigerator as I try to make sense of that ranking. "Ninety-seven in appetizers and side dishes?"

"Nope!"

"Um..." I pull out some mayonnaise, parmesan, a lemon, and artichokes. This is not a dip for the calorie-afraid. "It can't be ranked ninety-seven in all of cookery," I yell. I never rank that high.

"It's ninety-seven in the entire Amazon store."

The mayonnaise and parmesan fall to the floor with a thunk. Luckily, I'm able to cling to the lemon and artichoke hearts. "Don't tease me, Ash. I'm fragile." Unless we're talking about my hips. Those're about as fragile as a bulldozer.

"*Yummy Balls* is a bestseller in three categories," Ash says. "You got the little orange flag and everything!" The excitement in her voice is proof enough. She's not bullshitting me.

"Screen shot!" I yell. "Quick!" This has never happened to me before. Still clinging to my lemon and artichoke hearts, I run for the living room. "Where is *Tasty Dips?*"

"That one is ranked at a hundred and twelve. Your dips are lagging your balls, you slacker."

"Omigod. Omigod!" I flap my elbows, because ingredients in my hands. "I'm having a moment!"

She snaps my laptop shut. "See? There's your silver lining. You're going to earn thousands on your cookbooks this month."

But then reality sets in again, and I shudder. "Why bother with the cookbooks at all? I could just do porn. It obviously pays well."

Ash makes a sad face. "I'm just trying to look on the bright side."

"I know."

Suddenly, I *do* need sweet things. Maybe that's been the problem all along. I have misaligned my emotional crises with the wrong food response! Artichoke dip? What a disaster! No—I know what we need. And it's serious. This is not-fucking-around-anymore serious.

"We need chocolate," I say in a deeply terrified voice. "We need it right now."

"I could run to the store for you," Ash offers. "I was going to do that anyway."

"No need," I say with a sigh. "Put on an apron, though. You're helping."

21 HAPPY FACE STICKERS

Tom

I swear to God, as soon as I turn onto Lovett Street I can smell... chocolate? Chocolate. I'm not having a stroke. I really do smell it, and, as I walk toward her duplex (where the stairs really need to be repaired), the scent washes over me. It sort of mixes with the rosemary bush I'm holding.

Bush. Plant. Whatever. I stopped at the store for flowers, but then I saw these little Christmas tree plant things, and the poster said you could use the leaves in barbecue or something. It mentioned barbecue. Don't judge me.

I'm pretty sure that the last time I was in this neighborhood, there was no crowd of people milling around in front of a little old Victorian.

And the satellite news trucks are definitely a bad sign.

Fuck.

I stand there, fifty paces off, breathing in chocolate and the rosemary pine and panicking.

"Holy cow!" someone yells. The voice comes from behind me and then I hear the snick of a phone taking a picture. "It's Mr. Fixit! He's visiting his lady friend! And he's holding a bush!"

I turn around and smile, because really? What else is there to do? I could hold the plant in front of my face, try to tell whoever it is to fuck off, but I don't have the energy. And these are fans, not professional photographers, so telling them to fuck off would be plastered on social media. I can just see the live Facebook feed and all the hell that would bring.

It's tempting, actually. A quick end to my career and then I could stay here and be enveloped by chocolate. And Brynn.

Suddenly, I am enveloped, but it's not by either of the things I'd been hoping for. It's a pair of sharp, scarecrow, yoga arms threading around me and pulling my face down into a chest of augmented boobs. Goddamn plastic surgery. "Oh my god!" the woman squeals. "I love you so much! Judy, take our picture!"

Judy takes a series of pictures, and then I'm signing something. (Please let it not be a boob.) And I'm telling them how great it is to meet them. All the while, I'm planning evasive maneuvers. Because the news crew a few houses down is going to see me any second.

"I, uh, left my hammer in the car!" I say, apropos of nothing.

"You need that hammer!" the woman squeals. The pitch of her voice turns a few heads on the people standing down the block, and I'm spotted.

Fuckity.

"Gotta run nice chat!" I say over my shoulder as I take off running between two houses. I jump over a boxwood, and run past some nicely trimmed dwarf rosebushes and a napping Chihuahua. Which backyard is hers? I wish I'd looked more closely at the house. I pass two yards, and then a third. But the smell of chocolate gets very strong in the next yard, so I leap up onto the saggy little porch.

It really needs some new joists. I make a note to think about that later.

I pound on the door. "Brynn? It's me. Open up." My heart is in my throat. I can hear pounding feet behind me.

Then Brynn opens the door and grabs my bush for me.

That. Did. Not. Sound. Right.

"Are you okay?" she asks, when I am safely inside her entryway.

I don't have an answer for that, so I hold tight to her bush (the rosemary plant), and then just lean down and kiss her. She even tastes like chocolate. "Chocolate," I say out loud because I'm fucking smooth.

"Flourless chocolate cake," she says in a breathy voice, as if this explains everything. Actually, it does.

This woman. I need one more kiss, so I help myself. Her lips are soft beneath mine, and her body molds to my chest so perfectly.

I was having a really shitty day until just this second. But she kisses like a dream. My brain goes offline until she takes a step backward and looks up at me shyly. "Thank you for the rosemary."

"It's nothing."

"Did you get the video back?"

Fuckity.

"Yes and no." I sigh. "I now own the video, and my agent is slapping every website that posted it with a takedown notice. But social media has already spread it around pretty well. We're doing our best."

Her eyes get sad.

"My publicist has a few ideas, though." I shift my weight from foot to foot and put the shrubbery down on a kitchen counter. Laminate top, unfortunately. My favorite girl could use an upgrade.

I do this wherever I go—I mentally renovate every room I'm in. Can't shut it off. Occupational hazard.

"What ideas?" she asks.

Right.

"Can we sit down?" I ask her. This isn't a conversation for standing around the back door. Besides—there are knives in this room. She might use one of them on me after she hears my publicist's suggestion.

Brynn leads me through to a living room. The blinds are drawn, so it's dark. But I can tell the moldings are original and the plaster ceiling work is prewar. It's cute.

"Well, hello," her friend Ash says from the couch. "I just remembered somewhere I gotta be."

I've barely opened my mouth to greet her when she shoots out of the house with a blown kiss at Brynn, and vanishes. We hear the sound of camera shutters clicking, and Ash's voice saying, "Oh, fuck off. Unless you want to buy a house. Then come to mama."

The sounds die down, leaving Brynn and I eyeing each other in the dim light of the room. "So," she says quietly. "You were saying?"

A nervous chuckle escapes my chest. "Becky—my publicist—

95

thought that if there were a couple, uh, more respectable news stories out there about us, the, uh, video might fade."

"You mean..." When she frowns, the cute little forehead furrow returns. "Photos of us together, with our clothes on?"

"Yeah. That's a good start. The magazines would love that."

She chews her plump lower lip, and I'd like to chew it too. "What else?"

"Well..." I don't even know how to say it. "Becky thought..." I clear my throat twice in a row, but it doesn't get easier to say. "If you and I were engaged, it would be a big story. The media would run with it."

"Engaged?" she squeaks.

"Right. At least for pretend." I hate the word, honestly. And *fake-engaged* sounded even worse.

"We'd *pretend* to be engaged?"

"That's the idea. We'd let a couple of tabloids take our picture together. You know—smiling. With our clothes on. The slutty story becomes more banal. Then it's not two people fucking. Two people fucking is hot. It's two almost *married* people fucking, and who wants to see that?

"Okay. Good point. So we'd be fake-engaged until...? How does this resolve?" She crosses her arms under her delectable tits. It pushes them together a little, and my dick says, *I could just slide right between those babies* and I say, *Down boy!*—I hope to god not out loud.

The problem is that I don't actually know how this will end. Last year I'd tried to get for-real-engaged to a woman who I didn't like very much, and it turned out she didn't like me very much either, and she said no. The odds of convincing a woman I liked a lot to even *pretend* to be my wife were not that high.

The universe hates me. Obviously.

"Well, we'll pretend just until the worst of it blows over," I offer. "Until you get a job in your field, and some other poor fool's bare butt is seen flexing on the internet."

Brynn moans. It's not a sex moan, but my dick isn't a very good listener. He sits up and begs for another. *Moan again, baby* he says.

"I'm sorry," I say again. I am probably going to say it a thousand more times before this is over.

"It's not your fault," she says. "It's mine."

"What? No. That stupid party." Worst idea ever.

She puts a soft hand on my wrist, and I look down, liking the view. "I jumped you. It was totally out of character for me. And look what happened."

"Why did you, anyway?" The question has nagged me.

"Well..." Her cheeks turn pink. "I really wanted to. But first, Ash dared me." She smiles. "You know...actually..." Her eyes brighten, and she smiles. "Let's blame everything on Ash!"

"And Braht," I add, smiling back. "The party was his idea. I just went along with it."

We're grinning at each other like a couple of happy-face stickers. And then I remember my publicist's stupid idea.

Fuckity.

I clear my throat. "Publicist Becky is waiting for your answer. She needs to know how you want to play this. I'm happy to tell her where she can shove her crazy idea. But I thought I'd just run it by you first."

Brynn makes a face. "I just got out of a marriage. Pretending to get into another one is a terrible idea."

"Unless you want to make your ex jealous." The idea just pops out. It's my fragile male ego talking.

"Like my ex would even notice."

"Of course he will. If I were married to you, and then I lost you, the regret would be pretty intense."

Her face softens. "You are the nicest guy, Tom. If I ever wanted to be fake-married to somebody, you'd be at the top of the list."

It's the best compliment I've ever been given. Even better than the fan letter I got from a woman claiming that watching me operate a nail gun had given her an orgasm. I don't even want to know what Dr. Freud would say about that one.

"Any guess as to how long our fake engagement would last? Like, how long before it blows over? A week?"

I don't answer. I'm thinking.

"Two?"

Thinking is hard.

"More than a month?" Brynn asks me.

The answer arrives, thankfully. "The next season of my show is supposed to start filming in September. I'll be on location somewhere far away from here, and the tabloids will forget about us. When the season wraps up in March, my agent can release a line or two to the press that says you and I decided not to get married."

She licks her lips. "Does it help you if I play along?"

"A little," I admit. I don't want to tell her about Chandra, and getting dumped last spring. It's not a secret. It's just embarrassing. "You'd make me look like a family man and not a porn star. But I don't care, Brynn. You don't have to do this for me. Even if the network fires me under their morality clause, it's no big deal. I don't really care if season ten never gets made. I've had a good run."

Her eyes widen. "They can do that? They can fire you for having sex on the internet?"

"Sure. But even if they did, I'd get offers." *Not good ones, though.* Only this morning my agent fielded an inquiry from a cable station. They want me to do home renovations in the buff.

Seriously. Which TV genius decided that operating a table saw with your dick hanging out is a good idea?

"You don't need to worry about me. I promise," I assure her.

She puts her elbows on her knees, her chin in her hand. It's a pose of feminine reflection. "This idea sounds terrible. But I'm actually considering it. I don't want to be unhireable. College deans aren't as forgiving as TV."

I put a hand on her back. "I don't want you to be unhireable, either." The fact that she was even considering this crazy scheme lifts me in a way that surprises me. Last year I'd asked Chandra to marry me, and she'd said no. That stung a lot. For Brynn to claim me publicly seems incredible. Even if it's not real.

Gently, I rub her back. She's warm and solid under my palm.

Happy to take over, my dick offers.

You wish, pal.

"My blog got a record number of hits today."

"Really?" I laugh. "Of course it did. People are crazy. Your next blog post should be a spoof. Like, plate up two long slices of cake, one on top of the other. So it looks like they're..."

Brynn snorts and then giggles. I start laughing too.

"Or a carrot rising from between two potatoes." She laughs.

"Lots of melons!"

We lose it. And the sound of her laugh makes me hard. I pull her closer, my arm around her body.

Mine! shouts my dick, like a cranky toddler.

She's not, though. Reminding myself that our engagement is fake will be the hardest part. Okay, not the hardest part. That's in my shorts. The greatest challenge, then.

"Well, if we really tried this crazy scheme, how would this work?" she asks when we eventually stop laughing.

"Publicist Becky will put out a press release. We're very excited to announce our engagement, blah blah blah. Please respect our privacy."

"As if," Brynn grumbles.

"Yeah. I'm supposed to go to New York next week. You would come with me. We'll let some nice photographer snap our picture eating at a trendy restaurant."

She sits up a little straighter. "Which trendy restaurant?"

"You could pick," I say quickly. "Some place classy. We rehabilitate our image over food I can't pronounce. Whatever."

She smiles at me. "Won't they know it's a scam, though? I just met you."

"We have mutual friends," I point out. "The story is that we've been secretly dating since I arrived in Michigan."

"Which was...?"

"May."

"Good to know." She takes a deep breath and then sighs. "Okay. I'm in."

"Really?" I feel a lift in my heart that I'm going to have to examine later.

"Yeah. It's going to be weird, though." She gives me a sideways glance.

"Sure. Of course."

"We shouldn't have sex," she says in a matter-of-fact tone. "That will just complicate things."

"Right," I agree quickly.

My dick bursts into tears.

"It would be confusing," she says slowly. Her gaze is locked on mine. "To go at it like rabbits when we know it's, uh..."

"Throbbing," I offer.

"What?"

"Temporary," I correct.

"Right," she whispers.

"Right," I agree.

Then we lunge at each other anyway.

22 TODAY'S TOP TEN

Top Ten Reasons I Shouldn't Kick Off Our Fake Engagement by Sucking Face with Tom

1. I'm newly divorced. Like, the papers were finally signed just a few weeks ago.
2. I need to work on my self-worth.
3. Unbuttoning his shirt is taking time away from polishing up my résumé. But he looks really good bare chested on my sofa, his big legs spread...
4. Gah!
5. Other people are at work right now. At desks, with computers and pencil cups.
6. I need a real job.
7. Blogging about dips and balls is not a real job.
8. Because when I say the words "dips and balls" I giggle and think of Tom's dips and balls and I want more of them.
9. I am emotionally immature.
10. I'm unfocused and I need to fill my life with more things besides chocolate and fucking.
11. Omigod, I really want some chocolate and fucking. Not in that order.
12. When he plays with my boobs, I can't think.

13. There are reporters outside right now hoping to get this on camera.
14. But I have sturdy window treatments. I made them myself.
15. I can't even commit to writing a simple Top 10 List without fucking it up.
16. I'm a basket case.
17. I don't know Tom very well at all. What makes him tick? Is there anything in his past which should scare me away from being his pretend fiancée? Like, how did he get to be such a good kisser?
18. What the fuck am I doing? What number is this? What happened to my list? Why do I consistently start something, make a commitment, and then go all ass-askew on it and do my own thing? Why can't I focus? I want a better life, and a better life does not mean a better man

27) But why can't I have a man in my life? Don't I deserve that? I have to admit that there is something about him. About Tom. About his hands and his scent and the way he says "Molasses." Okay. He hasn't actually said "molasses," but I bet if I get him to say it, he'll chew that word. He is a man who loves to chew.

A) I totally want a real relationship, not a fake one.

TOP TEN REASONS I WANT TO BE IN A NOT-FAKE RELATIONSHIP
   1) Because I don't want to die alone.
   2) ...

23 I'M A BIG BOY

Tom

One time we filmed a "speed episode," where we renovated a house in a single weekend. It was a special project for a woman who was going into the hospital for amputation surgery. She needed a nice, safe, accessible house to come back home to. The pace was insane—my crew ripped out the kitchen cabinets and the bathroom fixtures all in the same hour. No breaks, no pauses to take a breath. It was the fastest, craziest thing I'd ever done.

Until today.

Brynn and I strip each other down on her couch at frantic speed. No lie, the Roadrunner would be envious. Before I know it, I'm sitting on her sofa, buck naked and lip-locked to Brynn. She's in my lap. We're still working on the last of her clothing, but it's hard to focus because of all the kissing. And the grinding.

Even through my lust fog, I realize Brynn was wrong about one thing. She said that sex would make things confusing right now. But I'm not the least bit confused. As I help untangle her from her leggings, the world makes more sense than it has all week.

Her creamy skin slides against mine, and then we're kissing again. I do my best impression of an octopus, touching her everywhere at once. Wherever my hands go, I find a new curve to cup, another smooth expanse of soft skin.

Our tongues tangle, jousting for control. I pull her further into my lap, and our hips lock together, her panties against my aching cock.

Yaaas, he gloats. *Finally.*

"This is a bad idea," she murmurs against my lips.

"No," I whisper, my mouth seeking her neck. "This is the best kind of idea."

"We're... It's just stress relief," she says, pressing closer.

"Of course," I babble as she grinds against me again. *Fuck.* I need her. Stress relief. So much stress. And I need so much relief.

I stroke my fingers across her belly, just above the elastic of her panties. But then she pulls away. *Why? Dear God, why?*

"Why?" I pant.

"Don't laugh. There are kittens on my underwear. I got them off of Mod Cl..."

Pussies on her pussy! my dick says, at least I hope it's my dick saying that and not me, because too much. The very idea of her themed panties does me in. Brynn is so cute and quirky. I just can't take it.

Our bodies collide again. I've never met anyone whose body lights me up like Brynn's does. We are closer together than fresh paint on primer, but somehow I get a hand between us. My fingertips slide down, down. I breech her kitten panties and tease her until she lays her head on my shoulder and shivers.

She makes me feel like a sex god.

"I went for years without this," she pants into my neck.

"Ten and a half days, honeybunch." But who's counting?

"No, b-before..." She can't finish the sentence because I tuck two fingers into her pussy and she moans. She's so soft and wet for me. "T-Tom," she gasps. "Do you have another condom?"

I am not a stupid man. "Of course." I take my hand back from its new favorite place and she curses under her breath. Quickly, I fumble for my shorts, which were cast aside on the sofa cushion. "Here." I hand her the condom just to see what she'll do.

She takes it with shaking fingers, tears open the packet. Then she slides off my body to give herself room to work. Now she's staring at my penis.

Come home, he says.

"Hey, sailor," she says. "Excuse me, I just really need to..."

She leans over and sucks the head of my dick into her mouth so quickly that I moan like a wildebeest. But, goddamn. She cups my balls and hums. And when she lifts her gaze to look me in the eye, it's a challenge not to humiliate myself. I wind her hair around my hand and quietly convert carpentry fractions into decimals. Three eighths is .375. Five eighths is...

She gives a good, hard suck.

"POINT SIX TWO FIVE!" I bellow.

Her mouth makes a popping sound as she releases me. "Come again?"

"I'm trying not to," I gasp. "Where'd that condom go?"

Now Brynn sheds her kitty panties. But somehow the break in the action makes her tentative again. Her eyes are wary, even as she hands me the condom and watches while I roll it down over my dick.

"Come here," I rasp, tugging her beautiful, naked self down onto my thighs. "You're too far away."

She sits up on her knees, and I position myself right below the door to heaven. She puts her hands on my shoulders and hesitates, her gaze bashful. "Should we go upstairs?"

"What?" My brain is gone. I'm millimeters away from sex. There is no question I could answer correctly right now unless the answer was supposed to be *YES YES YES NOW*.

"My bed is upstairs," she says.

I'm really not sure how that's relevant. "Honeybunch, I'll do you in your bed later. First you're going to bounce on my cock right here. So get busy." I slap her on the ass gently.

Her eyes widen, and she shivers. Her nipples are so erect they're practically weaponized. We're both as turned on as two people can be, so I palm both her hips and ease her down onto my ecstatic dick.

"Oh god." She throws her head back. "Oh fuck."

"That's the idea," I gasp. She's tight and hot, and I'm in heaven right now.

"Tom," she pants as she bottoms out onto my lap. "You make me say crazy things and do even crazier ones."

"I don't *make* you," I point out. "But I do encourage."

She leans in and kisses me. It's a good one, so I have to take

SARINA BOWEN & TANYA EBY

control of her mouth, pushing my tongue inside until we're both breathless. "I don't usually..." She sighs into my mouth.

"What?" I cup her breasts. They're so soft and pretty. "You do live alone, right?" I chuckle because it didn't occur to me to check before.

"Mmm hmm," she says, rocking her hips. It's amazing. "I...I'm not usually the aggressor."

"Pretty sure this was mutual," I mutter against her lips. "Ride me, honey." I roll my hips impatiently. But her eyes are wide, and I finally realize what the issue might be. It's the cowgirl position that's freaking her out. "Hey," I say, and my voice is a scrape. "You're doing great. You know that, right?"

She blinks, then gives me a bashful smile. Not for the first time I wonder about this Steve she used to be married to. *Seriously, dude. What were you thinking?* If Brynn was my wife (for real), I'd never put clothes on when she was around. Just in case. We'd have tried every position in the *Kama Sutra*. Even the silly ones.

Especially those.

She lays her head on my shoulder and takes a deep, steadying breath.

"Talk to me," I whisper, stroking her hair. "What do you need?"

"Can I ask you some questions?"

"Uh, sure?" I want to ask if it can wait until after I come, but I don't. I'm polite like that.

"I don't know anything about you." Her breath is soft against my neck. "But I just hopped right on your dick," she says. "*Again.*"

"Mmm. And I am so grateful. But what do you need to know?" I ask this in an almost normal voice. But I can't resist a little thrust. It just happens.

She moans, her lips grazing my jaw. "Okay," she pants. "When's your birthday?"

"January fourth," I gasp as my hips roll again.

"Capricorn...ungh," she says, beginning to ride me in small thrusts.

"Yeah." *Yes. Yes. Yes.*

"Dogs or cats?" she asks.

"Dogs," I say automatically. Because *doggy style* leaps into my brain.

She sighs as we find our rhythm. Her soft breasts brush my chest, and it's making me insane. "Favorite...color?"

That's a tricky one, because it really depends on the placement and the available lighting. "For what? I prefer warm neutrals in large rooms..." I kiss her so I don't have to answer the rest of the question, which could take all day. She whimpers when I stroke her tongue.

This is bliss. She's riding me like a champ, her soft curves rubbing me everywhere. My brain takes another vacation while she urges my body toward release. I'm not ready for it to end, though. I fight off my orgasm as her breathing kicks into high gear.

"Tom," she moans, and I brace myself. When she goes, I'm going with her.

"Yeah, baby?"

"How do you feel about white chocolate?"

What? The question penetrates my sex fog, because white chocolate is *ew*. "It's an abomination."

"Oh, yes!" she gasps, moving faster. "You are so..."

Whatever I am, it must be good, because she sobs out my name again as she comes, squeezing my cock and shuddering.

And I lose it too.

Two hours later we're curled up in her bed after round two, which followed a nap. I'm stroking one of her perfect breasts, and she's purring like a cat.

"So," she croaks, because we've been too busy fucking to speak. "We're just going to go at it like rabbits during our fake engagement?"

"If I have any say in it," I mumble. "Think how convincing we'll be."

She's quiet for a second. "This is a harebrained scheme."

"I never said it wasn't. But it's just dumb enough to work." And I really want to spend more time with Brynn, even under dubious pretenses.

"I want to help you."

"Don't do it for me, though. I'm a big boy."

Brynn blushes.

"I didn't mean my cock, but I'll take the compliment."

She rolls her eyes. "I should get up and make dinner. I'm hungry, so you must be starved."

I pull her onto my chest and take a nice long look at her naked body, and her cute little half-embarrassed smile. "We can just order pizza," I suggest. "Like the boring married couple my publicist is trying to make us into."

She smiles, and then kisses me.

24 TITS AND TOTS

Brynn

"I'm definitely not ready for a real relationship," I tell Ash and Sadie the next morning over breakfast.

I'd already had a nice sexfast with Tom. (That's breakfast after sex.) But I'd promised to meet my friends and a good girlfriend always sticks to her word. We have a Code of Honor. No matter what's happening in any of our sacks, we still show up when we say we're going to.

That doesn't sound quite right. Whatever.

At any rate, I kissed my fake fiancé goodbye a half hour ago and told him to lock up after he left. Then I snuck out the back door, just in case any photographers spent the night under my boxwood shrubs.

Now I'm at Marie Catrib's. It's a very granola kind of restaurant, but they have this breakfast that is tofu and zucchini and kale. And if you add a side of bacon, it's the perfect vegetarian meal. Except for the meat part.

"I'm not ready for a relationship," I say again, trying to convince myself.

Ash and Sadie don't answer me at first. They're feeding the babies. Not with their boobs. Sadie has sore nipples or something so she's bottle-feeding today. She has Amy in her arms and they both look so content. Ash is holding Kate, and they look like they're having a Spaghetti Western stare down.

It makes me laugh how uncomfortable Ash is with being maternal, but she helps out anyway when Sadie needs a hand.

I'd have fed the baby, but Ash and Sadie took one look at me and told me to eat. "Because you got the dick," Ash said. Even though I'd showered, she *knew*. And I was so hungry I was shaking.

So I am shoveling tofu and zucchini in my mouth, waiting for one of them to say something about this latest mess I've gotten myself into.

"I think it's done," Ash says.

"Kate," Sadie says. "The baby's name is Kate."

"It's looking at me. I think it wants something."

"I'm just going to go out on a limb here and guess that you and Hunter are never having children," Sadie says, her voice wry.

"Hunter can't actually get Ash pregnant," I point out. Since he doesn't actually exist.

"Which is incredibly convenient," Ash agrees.

Baby Kate makes another grumpy face at Ash.

"It hates me," she says.

"Try burping her," I suggest. A burp is a terrific idea, actually, so I let one rip. Daintily. Into my napkin.

"Nice," Ash says.

Sadie demonstrates the burping technique with Amy. Then Ash pats Kate's back until an enormous burp vibrates from the tiny body. "Ohhhhh. I like her," Ash says.

That's how you bond with Ash. You burp or fart without fear, then you're friends forever. It's pretty easy. She turns her attention to me. "What bullshit were you saying? I was ignoring you."

I love her so much.

"I'm not ready for a relationship."

"Why does it have to be a relationship?" Ash seems clearly confused.

"Ash, come on. I've..." I can't finish the sentence because I don't want to say *fucked* in front of the infants." So I whisper, "...*boinked* him two times."

Ash does not share my caution. "Two fucks does not a relationship make! Stop fucking stressing out about it!"

Sadie and I shush her. I mean, we are in a public place, no matter how granola Marie Catrib's is.

"I actually agree with you on this," Sadie adds. "You're not ready. A relationship takes a whole lot of work. It's exhausting. And when you have kids and he stops looking at you like you're a sexually desirable woman and instead treats you as if your only purpose on the planet is to feed your babies, give him dinner, and whack him off, I mean, that's a problem. Right?"

We don't reply. And if vinyl records were still a thing, and a needle-scratch could silence an entire restaurant of hungry people, that's what would be happening right now.

"I mean, hypothetically," Sadie offers lamely.

Ash and I share a troubled look. We know something bad is happening, but we also know that Sadie is so tender and fragile right now that if we push her one little tiny bit, she's going to take flight. She's in trouble, I think. Or at least her marriage is.

I take Amy from her so she can at least eat.

"Anyway..." she says, changing the subject while shoveling stuffed French toast into her maw. It's enormous, that French toast. Crisp on the outside, fluffy on the inside, smothering a mound of creamy goodness, and topped with sweet yet tart strawberries.

Ah. I think I just orgasmed right there. Again. My body is really on fire lately. I blame Tom. Sweet Tom. Sexy Tom. Tom of the man-hands and six pack and...

Goddamn it. I can't stop thinking about him. Even here, surrounded by food and my friends, my brain (and my loins) just keep thinking about him. The way he kisses. Smells. His throaty laugh. How we made love last night and then snuggled and then I...

Whoa. Whoa. Whoa. We did not make love. We screwed. Banged. Whatever.

This is bad. My subconscious is yearning for all those relationship perks. Maybe the fake engagement is the right move. It can feel like a relationship, but without any of the hazards. Such as a broken heart.

"Maybe everyone should try a fake relationship at some point or other," I reason.

Ash gives me a look that doubts my sanity. "Tell me again why this is a good idea?"

"No one wants to see an engaged couple screwing. It's like

watching your parents make out. So if we're engaged, then that porn scene is legitimate instead of trashy. We'll be fake-engaged until this whole thing blows over, okay? It's not nearly as cuckoo as it sounds! I swear!"

My credibility is tarnished, though, by a tear that leaks from the corner of one eye. Damned hormones.

"So you're fake-engaged," Ash repeats.

"I will be. I think so." I doth protest too much.

"And you don't want a relationship?" she asks, pinning me with her laser stare, the same one that causes couples to buy homes above their price range.

I nod carefully.

"Wow," says Sadie. "And this is good, right? Because you don't have any feelings for him, and it's totally okay with you to pretend a relationship so you're not actually invested in anything. And this will fix everything?"

I'm processing what she's saying, and my head is nodding. I'm pretty sure Ash laughs. Yep. She is laughing, because Sadie is laughing too, and then I'm laughing, because of peer pressure or something. "I just got divorced!" I say. "And now I'm engaged!"

We are howling. It's not really funny, so I'm not sure what is wrong with us. Hive mind or something.

After a minute or so, we all quiet down. I actually think I'm hyperventilating.

Ash says, "You're so screwed," and then I start crying. Real tears. Not crocodile ones. Sadie reaches for my hand and she starts crying. The babies start crying. The old woman in the corner eating a breakfast burrito starts crying. Even the server with the mohawk starts crying. Ash just looks at us, utters, "Oh, for fuck's sake," and asks for the bill.

25 OH HONEY

Tom

The only good thing I can say about the jewelry store is that it's not in a mall. I hate malls, with their recycled air and the smell of buttered pretzels.

And now I want a buttered pretzel, damn it. Ring shopping makes me want to stress eat.

"What are you muttering about?" Braht asks he parks his car in front of the shop.

"I hate shopping."

"You've mentioned that a dozen times in the past ten minutes. Stop whining. Get your big hairy butt in there and buy a ring, so we can golf."

"I hate golf."

"If that were true, you wouldn't beat me so often."

It *is* true, but beating Braht isn't all that tricky. And yet I'm nice enough not to say so. Much.

Braht bleeps the locks on his shiny blingmobile and I trudge toward the nicest jewelry store in West Michigan. I wouldn't want my fake fiancée to have anything less than the best.

As I walk in, I am nearly blinded by the flashing brilliance of hundreds of diamonds displayed under halogen lighting. Ow. My eyes hurt. But let's face it—that sting I'm feeling is really my ego. This is the same fucking store where I bought Chandra's ring six months ago.

It's déjà vu all over again as I cross the rose-colored (ugh! pink carpeting!) floor toward the counter in back, where they keep the luxury gemstones. And because my life is a bad dream on repeat, the same salesman is waiting. I remember that pink tie, chosen to match the decor.

And his nametag, which reads *Maynard*.

"Good afternoon!" he says, clapping his hands. "How can I help you fine gentlemen? Are you shopping for an engagement ring today?" He directs this question at Braht.

"Not me. Him." Braht points at me, and I scowl.

"But..." The salesman's chiseled face frowns in confusion. "I sold you a ring in the winter. Two-carat, round-cut center stone, with a halo setting adding a half-carat total weight!"

"That one was returned," I say through a clenched jaw.

"Oh, honey," he says softly. "I'm sorry."

"It's fine," I snap. "I have bad luck with women. My mother cursed me, I think." That extra bit just popped out, damn it. I'm probably jinxing my fake marriage by mentioning my mother right now.

Wait, can you jinx a fake marriage? I guess it doesn't matter.

"Women aren't the only choice, honey," Maynard says. "Maybe you're supporting the wrong team." He gives Braht the side eye. "You and your friend here would be hot together."

Braht doubles over with laughter.

"Not really," I tell Maynard over the howls of snort-laughter. "He's doing a vegetarian master cleanse. That gives you really stinky farts. It's all that dried fruit."

"Oh," Maynard says slowly. "What a shame."

"I know." I clear my throat. "Can we just get this over with? I need a ring. Not the same setting as last time."

"No! Of course not," Maynard agrees. "How about a solitaire for this go-round? Emerald-cut, perhaps."

"I was thinking a bezel setting," Braht says. "Platinum, of course. Don't show us any stone with a color rating below D, and S-range clarity."

"Naturally," Maynard agrees.

I just grunt.

Maynard grabs a set of keys large enough to break into Fort Knox and disappears into the back room.

"This is gonna be awesome," Braht says, rubbing his hands together. "Bling makes the world go round."

"No it doesn't," I argue.

"It's an expression."

"No it isn't." I should have gotten fake-engaged to Braht, because we already argue like an old married couple.

Luckily, Maynard comes back quickly. He sets a gorgeous velvet box on the glass counter. Then he puts one hand over the box and takes a deep, cleansing breath. "This is a very special diamond, men. Prepare to be dazzled." I kinda want to choke him already.

But then he opens the box, and I *am* dazzled. It's really glitzy, this rock. The setting allows the expensive jewelry-store lighting to shine right through the stone, so the ring appears to burst with color even though it's made from the whitest platinum and the iciest gem I've ever seen.

It's gorgeous. Absolutely perfect.

I hate everything about it.

Braht kicks me in the ankle, which is another reason we could never be a couple. "What's the matter? It's a great ring."

"Yeah. The greatest."

"So throw down the thirty grand, and let's roll. We could tee off in —" He checks his Rolex. "Twenty minutes."

I'm still staring at the ring. He isn't wrong. The simple setting means it's tasteful in spite of its size. But I can't look at this ring and not think about the last one I bought. Chandra's ring was flashier, because she's like Braht—she likes bling. It was a fucking *rock*. I'd wanted to make sure the TV viewers could see it clearly when we were on screen together. I'd really splurged on that sucker.

And it wasn't enough.

My throat is getting weirdly hot all of a sudden. I must be dehydrated. "Let's go," I rasp. "I'm not in the mood to buy a ring."

"Oh, honey," Maynard says. "Tissue?" He offers me a box.

"Nope. I'm good. Thanks for your help."

I get the hell out of there.

"What's your plan?" Braht asks as he puts his ball on the tee. Then he does some weird stretches which are supposed to improve your swing. He dangles the driver behind his body until it hits him in the ass.

It's taking fucking forever.

So I nudge him out of the way, step up to his tee, swing, and drive the ball about a million yards straight toward the flag. It flies through the bright blue sky for about a year before dropping onto the fairway and then bouncing onto the green.

Braht's jaw is dangling. "You hit my ball!"

"I needed to hit something. Seemed like the best option."

"But...it wasn't your turn."

We just glare at each other for a moment. I'm hanging onto my sanity by a thread here.

And maybe Braht gets that because he shrugs, grabs another ball out of his golf bag and tees it up. "Do you want me to just buy a ring for you?" he asks as he lines up his shot. Finally.

I wait until he swings, because that's polite. "No," I say as his ball sails toward...the water hazard. Shit. We'll be here all day. "I got it covered."

"With what?"

"A ring, Braht. I have one."

"Chandra's?"

"Nope."

"You can't use a fake, Tom. The media will sniff it out." He picks up his golf bag, and I do the same.

"It's my Great Aunt's ring."

"Jesus. Do you really want to go there?"

"Yeah." But I'll admit it's a strange choice. The ring is the only thing I have that belonged to a family member, since I don't have a family. Aunt Maddie and my grandmother were my only living relatives, and they both died when I was eighteen.

"Why do you want Brynn to wear it?" Braht asks. "Kinda precious, right?"

"Sure. But I'll get it back after we break up. And if I'm going to be fake-engaged to someone for a couple months, I might as well get some use out of it." I say this all glibly even though my throat is suddenly tight. Must be allergies.

Braht shrugs. "Saves you the restocking fee you were going to pay to return another rock at the jewelry shop."

"Right." I'd forgotten about that. Whatever.

"You can buy drinks tonight, then," Braht says, and I sigh.

"Let's just do some more damage to the little white ball."

"That's not exactly the point of golf," Braht warns, polishing his driver with a cloth he draws out of his pocket.

"It is today."

26 HORMONE SPIKE

Brynn

My suitcase is packed, and my girlfriends are blowing up my phone with advice-laden texts.

> *Ash: Don't even get dressed. Just stay naked the whole weekend.*
> *Sadie: She has to get dressed for good restaurants! And food trucks. Eating in New York is like consuming literature—go high or low. Michelin stars or street food. Skip all the stuff in the middle.*
> *Ash: How is that like literature? What?*
> *Sadie: Nabokov or 50 Shades.*
> *Ash: Ask Tom to get you tickets to Hamilton!*
> *Sadie: That's sold out three years in advance.*
> *Ash: But he's famous. Famous people can just snap their fingers and see Hamilton. It's a thing.*

From time to time I glance at their stream-of-consciousness advice. But for once I'm not really listening. In the first place, there are a lot of places that needed waxing and shaving before my New York adventure. I plan to be as soft as an angel food cake.

Now I kind of want a slice of angel food cake, damn it.

I've painted my toenails an edible shade of peach, and styled my hair. I'm ready. And—this is the crazy thing—I'm *excited*. Even if this trip is completely bogus, it's really nice to be taking a vacation from my own life. I could be sitting here this week worrying about finding a job, hoping I'll get some responses to my job query emails and posts on those electronic application sites. The new semester starts soon, so I'm basically running out of time for finding a job this year.

Deep breaths. Deeeeeeeeeep brrrrreaths.

There's nothing I can do about those applications now. If I stay home, I'll literally be pacing in circles and occasionally posting new recipes to my blog. But instead of pacing and waxing neurotic, I'm flying to New York with my fake fiancé to have our picture taken for the tabloids. It's ridiculous.

It's a blast.

I'm making good choices.

Goodish.

Tom will pull up any moment to take me to the airport.

Just because it's a fake engagement, doesn't mean we can't have some real sex. When Steve proposed, we didn't have sex that night because he had a cramp in his toe. He needed more potassium, he said, and he ate a giant banana, but that sort of doused the mood. So I'm going to do this engagement right.

I put on some new lingerie that Ash and I shopped for. It's basically made up of strings, but Ash assures me it's very trendy. A girl can't wear her granny panties to New York. I adjust my strings and slip on a wrap dress because Tom seems to like them. Or rather, he likes undoing them. It occurs to me that with the wrap dress and all these lingerie strings, I've turned myself into a big old present. Happy Birthday, Tom. I should jump out of a three-layer cake.

Now I want three-layer cake.

When I hear an engine outside, I slip on a pair of sandals and a little cardigan. I'm ready for adventure.

Tom's Big Shiny Truck has pulled up at the curb, and I practically gallop toward the door and wrestle my bag outside. I give him the finger.

Wait, that sounds wrong.

I hold up an index finger in the universal sign for "Just a minute, fake fiancé, I'll be with you as soon as I lock my door."

But Tom doesn't wait. He leaps out of his Big Shiny Truck and comes up the sidewalk.

"Sorry," I say, fumbling with my keys. "We're not late, though."

"Of course not," he rumbles, kissing my cheekbone. He looks at me and his fingers seem to move toward the tie at my side. He pats my body like he's eager to unwrap me later.

That one move makes me quiver.

"It does, does it?" he asks, and I realized I'd said that out loud.

I need to take an Ativan. Air travel, hot man, fake engagement, tabloid pictures, and New York have made my hormones spike.

Tom picks up my bag and carries it to the truck for me. His arm muscles flex as he lifts it into the back seat.

Oh.

Wow.

I could get used to this.

On the way to the airport, I indulge in thoughts of hotel sex with Tom. The truck hums along the highway, and I'm humming right with it. Maybe it's all that horsepower.

Or maybe it's Tom. He's flipped some kind of sexual switch in me that I can't shut off.

"What are you thinking about so hard over there?" he asks.

"Hotel sex." There's really no point in lying.

"Mmm," he says, and his tone approves.

But then it occurs to me. "You've probably had lots of hotel sex." For me this will be exotic. But if I understand his job correctly, he must be in hotels all the time.

"Mmm," he says again, and the sound vibrates in my chest. And other places. "But I haven't had any hotel sex with you."

There are lots more vibrations now. Yowza.

Tom parks the Big Shiny Truck in the parking garage at Gerald Ford International Airport. You can't actually fly outside the country from this airport, but the name sounds better than Gerald Ford Small Potatoes Airport.

I've already got my door open when Tom grabs my hand and gives it a squeeze, stopping my progress. Right away I'm thinking, *Why not a quickie in the truck?* I close my door.

"Brynn," he says quietly.

"Yes, Tom?" I breathe. *Take me. The wrap dress will make this easy. Just one little pull and I'll unravel at your feet.*

"This is your last chance to bail out of the fake engagement before it starts making headlines. I'd understand."

Oh. "That is very considerate of you. But I'm along for the ride, okay? I'm not exactly famous for my good decision making. But here we are outside a fake international airport, and I've painted my toenails for this occasion so let's be fake engaged."

He grins at me like I'm hilarious. "Okay. You're going to need this, then." He pulls something out of his pocket.

Oh, fuck. It's a ring box.

He's doing this. He's doing this now right by the curbside check-in and a woman saying in her thick Michigan accent, "Oh, fer sure, I hope the plane ride doesn't make me nauseous, dontcha know?"

"Brynn?" he asks, and suddenly everything else around us silences.

Something goes a little wrong with my breathing, because this part is weird. There's no denying it. When you get out that little square velvet box and hand a ring to a girl, it's supposed to mean something. It's supposed to be a moment.

I'd forgotten how it felt to see that box. It feels like potential.

"Breathe, honey," he says.

Right.

I breathe. It's more of a hiccup, really, but then I try again. He holds my gaze, and his eyes tell me that he knows this is weird. "I hope it fits." He opens the box and sighs.

The ring inside is beautiful. It's not like anything I've ever seen before. Smooth gold surrounding a simple, frosted orb. It's not a diamond, which is great because diamonds always look like just glass to me. This globe thing seems luminescent. I love it to pieces.

Shit!

I love it. And I want it on my hand now. And maybe always.

"It looks vintage," I say to cover up my own yearning. It occurs to me that there is no way he found something like this at a jewelry store chain. He removes the ring and slips it onto my left hand. It floats onto my finger. "It fits. Wow," I say stupidly. Do *not* cry, I order myself. I refuse to make this any weirder than it already is. "It's so pretty. It will be, uh, no hardship to wear this for a little while."

"It's a moonstone," he says, "It..." He stops and I wonder what he's going to say next. "It's not a big deal."

"It looks like a big deal," I whisper. "Like a treasure."

His big brown eyes soften. "You're the treasure here." He leans over and kisses my forehead. "Anyway, we have a flight to catch."

I look at the ring, and I'm sort of bursting inside. I want to ask him where he found it, but I can tell he doesn't want to talk about it. And this is the perfect ring. It's so *me*. And I can't even say so. I can't tell Tom how much I love it, because it's never going to be mine.

And neither is he.

Tom takes my hand in his. He admires the ring on my finger. I feel the weight of his gaze, but his expression is completely unreadable. Then he curves his hand over mine, and the ring disappears from view. "Thank you," he says quietly. "Now let's go to New York."

27 FLYING HIGH

Tom

Usually, I fly to New York in business class. It's only a couple of hours to get there. There's a little more legroom in business than in coach, and a guy like me can use that, and it's a little less pretentious than first class. I've never been a suit-and-tie kind of man. I'm a dusty jeans and T-shirt dude.

But today, with Brynn, I've sprung for the first-class cabin. She seems delighted by this and that makes me...well, delighted too, I guess.

"Oh, they give you blankets!" she cries as we reach our seats. Then she unfurls one. "Blankets for little, tiny people!"

"Or an arm," I say. "I find that one arm always has the vent blowing on it, so it's really useful for that." She snuggles in next to me, and I wouldn't mind if there was a little *less* room in first class, if you know what I mean. Just one little tug on that bow on the side of her dress and she'd be naked.

I shift in my seat. Feels a little less...roomy in here all of a sudden.

When we are buckled in, the flight attendant, Tish, brings us two glasses of champagne. (Easily arranged beforehand by my publicist Becky.) "Congratulations, you two!" Tish drawls.

Brynn has this big smile on her face that doesn't quite ring authentic, but it's okay. We clink glasses and say cheers. "Would you mind..." I say quietly to Brynn once she's taken a sip of the not-exactly-cheap champagne. It's harder to ask than I imagined. She looks at me, perplexed. I try again. "Can I, uhm, post a picture? Of your hand?" She still looks confused. "With the, uh, ring on it? So that...you know...*followers*," I say, hoping she gets what I mean. This is humiliating. Why did I ever listen to Becky? It's because of all her fucking exclamation points. These were her instructions:

Make sure you take a pic! Of her ring! To show you're engaged!!! But don't say you're ENGAGED, obvs, cuz social media will do that for you! Keep the MYSTERY!!

Eesh.

I snap the photo of Brynn's hand holding the glass of champagne, and I caption it "Flying High." With a filter, that fucking ring practically glows. Oh, it does without the filter too.

Weird.

I hit the little button to post it. Becky says by the time we land, the whole world will know about my engagement. Our engagement. My engagement to Brynn.

Fuck!

My *fake* engagement to Brynn.

Then, out of nowhere, my dick whispers, *Fake or not, she's miiiiiine.*

He's a creepy fucker sometimes.

Brynn

I'm in the middle of a fairy tale. Usually at this hour I'm curled up on the sofa eating cheese nips and looking at cookbooks, all while lamenting my lack of a teaching job in September. But today? Today, first class, a beautiful ring, champagne, New York...Tom. This can't be real! It's too great to be real!

And, of course, it's not real.

This was such a stupid idea.

Why did I agree to this? How is this going to fix anything? No one is going to care that we're engaged. The schools I'm applying to won't even notice. All they'll see is Naked Writing Professor, which, honestly, shouldn't be too surprising because writing teachers are always a little bit hippy-ish.

Part of my brain is like, *Take an antidepressant*, and the other part is like, *Just shut up and enjoy this weekend*.

I don't know which part to listen to.

When the plane lands, and I loosen my death grip on Tom's leg—fear of flying anyone?—we're the first ones down the jetway. As soon as we disembark, there are people pointing iPhones and cameras at us. Before I can even process how reporters got past security, Tom gives me a little tug and shows me his phone. It's vibrating maniacally.

Then I look at my phone and there are so many tweets and shares of his ring post that I just keep scrolling and scrolling and scrolling. "What the fuck?" I breathe.

"Told you I'd fix it," he says, all proud.

I look at him with a little bit of awe, and by awe, I mean with my jaw hanging wide open and my eyes all huge and possessed...and that's the picture that lands on the gossip page of the *New York Post*.

28 SVENKA & TORVOLD

Brynn

I thought that my first-class seat on the jet was fancy. As it turns out, the plane ride was just the hors d'oeuvre. When Tom opens the door to the main course—our suite at the Mandarin Hotel in Columbus Circle—I literally gasp.

"Wow," Tom say. "It's so—"

"Beautiful!" I say at precisely the same moment Tom says "hideous."

"But..." In the living room, I practically sink into the custom circular rug underfoot. The decor is severely modern—curved walls in grays and purples, with silver flourishes. The sofa isn't just a sofa. It's most of the circle. And, fine, it does resemble something I'd expect to find on a spaceship.

That doesn't dim the appeal of this room, though. The view is spectacular. All of Central Park is laid out before us. And tonight the buildings surrounding the great green rectangle will light up in every direction. I stand in front of the floor-to-ceiling window and try to take it all in.

Behind me, Tom carries our bags through to the bedroom. When I follow him, I find another stunning view in two directions. And the bathroom! It's enormous and has more gizmos than a bathroom needs. "Tom! There's a TV screen embedded in the mirror. Just in case you really need to poop during those final minutes of the big game." I giggle.

And when I gallop back into the bedroom Tom follows me with dancing eyes. "I'm glad you're impressed." He nudges me out of the bedroom towards the oddly shaped sofa. I sit down and he drops down beside me, pulling me in, kissing me on the eyebrow. "You are fun. But that light fixture looks like something from planet Naboo."

"But that's just it," I say, climbing aboard his lap to straddle his great muscular thighs. "That's why it's excellent. We're never going to live here. But we get to visit this planet as forty-eight hour guests, and be fabulous in an entirely fake way."

Heck, I could be talking about our relationship or the hotel. Take your pick.

"This room is for…" I pause to think of the right names. "Svenka and Torvald. They have a TV in their bathroom mirror at home, and an espresso maker in that shade of puce."

"Oh, baby." His expression softens, and I feel like I've just won the lottery. The way he looks at me turns me to goo.

"What?" I breathe.

"I *love* that you know the color puce."

We kiss again, and he grins against my mouth. "Okay. You're right. This is fun. But I have trouble walking into a room without mentally renovating it."

"Take the night off, Torvald."

"I'll try." He puts one thick finger in the V of my wrap dress. "But I have to draw the line somewhere. If I try to do you on a circular couch, we'll both end up with curvature of the spine."

It would probably be worth it. Nobody has ever spoken to me like Tom does. Like I'm sexy. *If I do you.* He makes it sound so casual.

I want to be *done.*

"Svenka is wearing very complicated lingerie," I warn him. "Torvald is going to need a few minutes to free her." Maybe the rope-like set was a bad idea. I don't want to waste any of our valuable time.

"It's probably just as well. Torvald has a meeting with his handlers in twenty minutes."

"No!" He'd warned me about that damn meeting, but I hadn't listened. Maybe he could be late. I put my hands on his broad shoulders and squeeze. "Twenty minutes is plenty of time," I whisper. Then I hike my body closer to his and rise up on my knees so that my boobs are right in his face.

He groans, and his eyes practically roll back in his head. "Twenty minutes isn't enough, though. I'm gonna take my time with you." He nudges the shoulder of my dress aside, getting a glimpse of the strappy bra I'm wearing. "Damn, Svenka."

"That's what I hoped you'd say."

He takes another peek, and he doesn't have to say anything, because his dick is doing the talking. It's almost as if I can hear his dick speaking to me.

Weird.

He does this sexy little grunt thing and actually bites his bottom lip. A man biting his bottom lip on the dance floor while doing the sprinkler: decidedly unsexy. A man I'm straddling biting his lip because he's trying to control himself? Swoonworthy. Oh, wait. He's saying something. I wasn't paying attention.

"What?"

"While I'm gone, you have a big decision to make."

"Dinner?"

He shakes his head slowly. "You have to choose — the bed, the walk-in shower, or the footstool."

My mouth goes dry as my mind fills suddenly with multiple images of me being done in various positions. "I only get to choose *one?*" The last word is a squeak.

He grins. "The meeting I'm having will probably stress me out. So pick something good for before dinner. The runner-up can be for afterward."

Now I'm quivering everywhere. "Does Torvald have a preference?" I'm playing with fire right now. I don't really want to make him late to his meeting. But I can't resist poking the beast.

He makes a hungry growl. "I can see benefits all around. I want you in that shower, all wet and slippery..."

Jesus. Knowing me, I'll probably slip and kill myself, though. "Or?"

"When it gets dark, I'm gonna put you on your hands and knees in front of that window and bang you in front of the city lights."

I let out a little whimper and then kiss him. He wraps his arms around me, and as I kiss him, his nice, hard dick thickens up beneath me. "Mmm," I murmur. "That's it. I pick that. A *do* with a view!"

He kisses me with those generous lips. But then I feel him snort. And then he throws his head back and laughs. "You're the view, honeybunch. Thank you for making my New York trip more fun."

His smile makes my heart happy and sad at the same time. It's going to be really hard not to fall for this guy for real. I think I already have.

Tom goes to his meeting on time, damn him. I'm left alone to amuse myself in my favorite city in the world. Oh, the hardship.

I start by taking myself to Bouchon Bakery. It's in the same big complex as the hotel, so Svenka doesn't even need to step into the July heat for her exquisite pastries. I buy three pastries to go and bring them back to the room to photograph for my blog. But after I compose some rather lovely photos in front of the window, I've only killed a half hour.

So I eat one of the pastries, because it's terrible to waste food.

I still have at least an hour before Tom returns. He's off talking to his agent about the next season for his TV show. Apparently they've been waiting for him to make some big decisions about the show, but I haven't asked for details because I don't want to pry.

That doesn't mean I'm not curious, though. So I sit down in the center of the C-shaped sofa, leaning against a silk pillow that probably retails for three hundred bucks. I aim the remote at the giant flat-screen TV on the opposite wall and I sort through the menu options until I find exactly what I'm looking for. *Mr. Fixit Quick*, season nine.

I'd rather start with season one, because sometimes you need to see narrative from its beginning. But season nine is the only one on offer, so it'll have to do.

The intro is splashier than I expect it to be. There is a montage of a house going up in fast forward, and a jaunty piece of music arranged for acoustic guitars. When the camera pans onto Tom, seated at a desk, I'm not really ready. Even though I knew he had a successful TV show, I'm still taken by surprise when his face appears, larger than life, in all its handsome glory on the screen.

My fake fiancé is really photogenic. Wow.

The episode begins with Tom evaluating an old house somewhere in Virginia. He runs his broad hand over an oak banister while admiring the prewar architectural details with the homeowner. "We're going to save what's beautiful about this house, while making it into a more functional family home."

"That's amazing," the woman on the screen tells him. But her eyes are saying something else. Something like: *I want to scale you like one of the old chestnut trees on my property line*.

That's when the truth hits me like a ton of bricks. When I look at Tom, I already see a man who's out of my league. But now I realize it's so much worse than that. There's an entire *nation* of women for Tom to choose from. All those viewers admiring his power drill in hi-def. In their hearts they already feel like they know him, the same way my mother talks back to the shopping network hosts, as if they can hear her.

Guess what? I can get the word *relationship* right out of my head. Because I never had a chance.

This realization should depress me, except I'm watching some quality TV. And also, I have two pastries left. But I'm not eating them. It's just comforting to know they're there.

The first episode outlines a plan for the house. His working crew comes in and demolishes the old kitchen. The female homeowner looks a little horrified as a giant hole opens up in the side of her home.

"Take that, lady." I giggle. The second pastry disappears from the bakery bag, and I barely even register eating it. I mean, it was right there a second ago.

In the second episode, our homeowner looks less unsettled. No—she's practically enraptured by the kitchen Tom builds for her. And so am I. This woman gets the marble-topped baking station that I've always wanted. She has a forty-two inch Sub-Zero and a Wolf range.

I officially hate her.

In fact, that might be the point of this show.

There's one other character, though, that I hate a little bit more. Mr. Fixit Quick has his very own decorator. Even her name annoys me—Chandra. She's thin and beautiful, and she apparently gets paid for choosing all the furniture and color schemes on Tom's show. She picks a sage green for the cabinets. It looks fabulous, which makes me loathe her. And then she finds the most adorable barstools to line the new counter space.

Grumpy now, I eat the last pastry, because fuck it.

It's hard to put a finger on my instant dislike for the decorator. She's too skinny, for one. If Chandra ever visited Bouchon Bakery, she definitely did not eat three pastries. She probably wouldn't even breathe inside the bakery in case calories are airborne. I also don't like her hair. She's too blond. I hate blondes.

But my good friend Ash is very blond, and I don't hold it against her. I love her hair.

Hmm.

It isn't until I watch episode three, when the Virginia home is finally done, that I realize why I hate Chandra more than the woman who gets to live with this new kitchen. It happens when Chandra chooses a color for the Virginia woman's big dining room china cabinet. Big deal, right? Any hack can choose a paint color called "Deep Coral."

It's just that Tom's face lights up like a neon sign when he sees the end result. Tom is impressed with Chandra. He smiles at her like she's a member of the club. And she totally is, damn it. I'll bet she's at Tom's meeting right now, spouting off color names and looking skinny. She has a great job and can write off her salon visits as a tax deduction.

I have no job, and my only claim to fame is an accidental porn clip.

I almost turn off the TV and fall into a deep depression. But just as I'm lifting the remote, Tom fills the screen again. I can't shut that off. Not when he's wearing a tool belt and a tight T-shirt. And the camera does a close-up, as if knowing I'm here on the edge of my seat. The cotton clings to his pecs as he slams his palm against a misbehaving piece of lumber. *Bad lumber, bad.* He's so yummy. When the board has taken its spanking, he reaches down to pick up a power drill. Bracing himself against the wood, he tenses his impeccable biceps, pulls the trigger and—

Drills things. Over and over. He presses the big, fat drill bit against the wood and... Drills it.

"Holy mother of God," I pant as his poor T-shirt stretches to accommodate this labor. His big Man Hands are busy on the screen. I can see the masculine hairs on the backs of his hands in high-def. And I want those hands on my body. Right now, preferably.

I sink into the weird sofa and moan.

29 EXCLAMATION POINTS!!!

Tom

I'm both horny and grumpy, and that's a rough combination.

It doesn't help that traffic sucks. And I'm not even in a car. I'm hoofing it in Midtown, trying not to bounce tourists out of my way as I head for my agent's office on Fifty-third Street.

"Tom!" my agent shrieks when I finally reach her office. Like I'm her long-lost puppy. "Hi, honey!" She grabs me and kisses me on both cheeks.

"Hey, Patricia." Her cuddliness is the first sign that something is wrong. She's a New Yorker through and through—she'd rather kill you for your parking spot then kiss you. Also, I'd been bracing myself to schmooze the producer of my show, but he isn't here yet. "Where's Samuel?"

Patricia sits heavily in her giant leather chair and makes a tent of her fingers.

Uh-oh.

"Samuel isn't coming. We don't need him today."

"We don't? I thought we were signing off on the details for season ten today. If that's not the case, then why am I even here?"

Patricia's hand strays to her favorite desk ornament, which is a tiny but accurate reproduction of the guillotine used to decapitate

Marie Antoinette. I bought it for her as a tool to shave the ends off the Cuban cigars she smokes.

Lost in thought, she moves the lever up and down a couple of times with her fingertip, and I brace myself. "This is very unusual. But the network is considering releasing you, based on the morality clause in your contract," she says slowly. "It's foolish of them, and I'm trying to talk them out of it."

"Those bastards!" My gut clenches, and I actually see red. A serious red. Like Benjamin Moore's Vermillion. "I didn't do anything wrong. Having sex in your own home is not amoral."

She nods, her finger executing a few more invisible Frenchmen before she folds her hands. "But the contract says they can release you for negative publicity related to your personal life. It doesn't say they can release you only if you're truly a pervert."

"Then fix it!" I bluster. "I signed this thing in the first place because you approved the language."

She flinches. "We're doing all we can. Publicist Becky is on her fourth espresso this morning, and my legal team has been shooting down stray copies of that video for seventy-two hours straight. And we're doing all we can to push the story that you're engaged and that you're not a pervert."

Slowly, I unclench the fists I've made. "They can't push me off season ten for this. That's bullshit." Even as I say these words, I hear my own hypocrisy. Half an hour ago I was dragging my feet on shooting season ten. I didn't want the network to rush me. But the fact that they might fire me instead is unacceptable.

Diva, much?

"Let them work through their issues," Patricia says. "They're going to run some teasers for season ten—shots of an old house. A picture of you looking wholesome with your hammer." She snorts. "Okay, maybe not a hammer. A belt sander. Anyway, they'll float your face out there and see what happens. When there's no backlash from the bible belt, they'll man up and schedule the season."

"Or they'll look at the rest of their lineup and realize they still need my ratings numbers to peddle to their advertisers."

"Exactly," she agrees.

For a hot second this bit of bluster gives me a second wind. But then I realize something. "If this works, I'll have to actually shoot season ten fairly quickly."

"Of course. But you live for this shit." Patricia grins.

I used to, anyway. "We'll have some hiring to do first. We need a new designer."

The smile slides off Patricia's face. "Not necessarily."

"What?" She can't be serious. "I can't have Chandra on the set. She won't want the job anyway."

"Well…" She clears her throat. "The job has to be offered to her. The network has to prove that she wasn't let go for turning down your offer of marriage. Plus, she really won't want the job now that you've 'moved on.'" I swear she puts that last bit in quotes. Patricia knows this business. She knows we're in crisis mode and that not every relationship is as it seems. Something I know too well.

My temples throb suddenly. When Chandra broke up with me after, episode ten, she'd told me I was just a "stopping point" on her path to stardom. She didn't want to settle down and "play house." She had bigger, better things to do.

Not bigger! my dick protests. *Have you seen me?*

"It will probably turn out okay," Patricia says. "All of it. The network will realize the error of its ways, and Chandra will turn down the job. Stay calm, hot buns." She rises. "Let's go see your cheerleader. I mean, Becky." I think that was Patricia's attempt at humor.

A root canal sounds more fun. But I follow her anyway.

Publicist Becky is twenty-two going on twelve. Even while we're talking in her office, she's on social media. I think her pink phone might be surgically attached to her hand.

"You and Brynn make the cutest couple!" she gushes after hanging up with her latest caller. "*People* and *US Weekly* both want exclusives! Two covers! It's gonna be rad!"

"But…" I do the math. "If you give them both the interview, it won't be exclusive." Then I remember I don't really care. "What do I have to do?"

"Just be yourself! You're Tom Spanner! Women love you! You're a good guy, Tom! Look, I can prove it." She tap dances past me and out of the room, and after a beat I get up and follow. In the hallway, she yanks open a closet, and inside there are stacks of file boxes. Publicist Becky rips the top off one and sort of throws it backward.

I catch it.

"Look!" She turns around, clutching two handfuls of letters. She shoves a couple of them into my hands. They're addressed to me, care of the network. They've been slit at the top, since interns read all my fan mail. I pull out a letter on pink stationery.

Tom—

Pick me! I'm 5-4, 138 pounds. Thirty-four years old. My boobs aren't as perky as Chandra's but they are real. That woman is crazypants, okay? I'm single and I'd never kick you out of bed. If you'd have gotten down on one knee in front of me I would have peed myself from excitement. You're the best, and I would love to be your wife.

Love, Candi

P.S. When I said I would have peed myself, that was just an exaggeration. I don't really have any issues with incontinence. Not often, anyway. Call me!

I look up at Publicist Becky, whose hands are still brimming with letters. "See? These started showing up last March, and never stopped. And now the women are all hot and bothered by your pumping backside. That engagement ring picture only confirms you're honorable...and...well... All those boxes are filled with marriage proposals! For realz! We're sending everyone who offers to marry you a *Mr. Fixit Quick* keychain, and a coupon for twenty percent off at Home Depot."

Looking over Becky's shoulder, I count the file boxes. There are at least a dozen. And I don't even know how I feel about that. It's really flattering. Then again, it just proves that our nation is full of women willing to propose to a man they've never met.

Becky grabs the letters out of my hand, hurls it back into the open box, kicks the closet door shut, and frog-marches me back to her office. My head aches as she outlines all the photos she wants of me and Brynn, and her sunny outlook for my rehabilitated reputation.

"I did have one big new idea!" she chatters. "Nobody can resist a hard-luck story! I think it's time we did an interview about your childhood! Heck! We could take a camera crew to the trailer park where your ailing grandmother raised you!"

"Manufactured housing site," I mutter. Then I catch myself. "Just stop right there. We aren't doing that. If you try to play the Crappy Childhood card, I will fire you."

Becky sits back in her chair and puts the phone down for the first time. "No need to go nuclear, Tom. If you don't like my plans, you can just say so."

As if. "I'm engaged because of you. Fake-engaged."

Her smile returns. "But you're doing it beautifully!"

Eventually I'm allowed to leave and return to the hotel. I'm in dire need of a cocktail and a sandwich.

And Brynn. A smile from my new favorite girl will go a long way. Let the healing begin.

As I approach the door to our room, I hear the TV on inside the room. At least I hope it's the TV, because otherwise someone is operating a table saw inside our hotel suite. I'd know that high-pitched whine anywhere.

I wave the key card in front of the scanner, and when the light turns green, I push the door open. "Hi, honey, I'm home!" I call out. Because I've always wanted to say that.

Brynn is on that weird couch. She jumps like I've startled her, and then grabs the TV remote and kills the screen immediately. In the silence, I notice a few details. Her cheeks are rosy, she has crumbs in her hair, and her bosom is heaving. She looks up at me, and the sex haze she's fallen under is like a beacon. My body responds immediately to her flushed face and her "do me" eyes.

"Whatcha watchin?" I ask slowly. I kick the door shut and toss the key card onto a table. When I take a step toward the sofa, her breath hitches audibly.

"P-porn," she whispers, her eyes guilty.

"I knew I liked you."

30 A BONDING EXPERIENCE

Brynn

When Tom enters the room, I'm ready for him. I've just spent the last two hours fantasizing about his various body parts holding various tools and banging around construction sites.

He's a hot guy and I'm a big girl and this is just a sexcation we're having together. Torvald and Svenka. Let the banging commence.

Tom kicks the door shut and crosses quickly to the sofa. "Did you make a choice?" he asks, and his voice is pure gravel.

For a second I have no idea what he's talking about. But then my inner Svenka kicks into action. "Bed," I whisper.

No sooner is the word out of my mouth when Tom leans over and scoops me off the sofa, his hands under my ass. I wrap my arms around him to make the job easier. I'm not just some tiny waif you can toss around.

Although now I get it. Having just watched Tom carry everything from a water heater to a hearty stack of two-by-fours, it's less shocking that he can pick me up and fling me around.

And fling me he does. My ass hits the puce bedspread seconds later. Then I'm sitting there staring up at his powerful Paul Bunyan body. Confession: the fact that he can make me feel small is a big turn-on.

He leans down, plants those big hands on the bed and kisses me with generous lips. I'm already turned on, and he's ready to roll. So we attack each other's mouths like starving people. Tom gives a deep groan as he tastes me for the first time. "Can't wait to fuck you," he says against my mouth.

His deep, manly voice gives me a full-body shiver. No one has ever talked to me as if I was desirable. No one. Steven treated me with indifference. And the few lovers I had before him were all very gentle.

It seems wrong to gripe about gentleness. But Tom's big hands aren't so careful as he tilts my head to perfect our connection. The way he touches me is a revelation. He makes me feel like it's okay to crave this.

Svenka likes it a little rough sometimes. Who knew?

"Missed you, baby," he says, straightening up.

Now I'm eye level with his belt buckle. So I reach up and undo it with eager fingers. I unzip him too. And his erection is right there, hard and stretching against the cotton of his underwear. He looks uncomfortable in there. So I do what's necessary—free him by pushing the offending fabric out of the way. His very hard dick stands up straight, and it's almost like a salute.

I salute him back, because that's just polite.

Tom chuckles. "See anything you want?"

Do I ever. I want... "Your cock," I breathe. Because Svenka would say it aloud.

"Where do you want it?" Tom asks. Then he puts one of those wide hands on top of my head and gathers my hair into his hand. "Suck me, honey," he says.

Top 10 Truths Learned While Giving Tom a BJ

1. I would have thought that Tom ordering me to blow him would feel demeaning. But it's really just hot.

2. And anyway, if I didn't *want* to use my tongue to lick him from base to tip, he'd be fine with that. I trust Tom. Fuck, I really do. That's why I'm treating his penis like my favorite ice cream flavor

right now. And his moans are better than a double scoop of coconut almond fudge.

3. When I named my blog Brynn's Dips and Balls, I was really onto something.

4. I haven't done this in a long time. But Svenka somehow knows what to do. It's just like riding a bike, right?

5. Tom's dick tastes much better than a bike. When my tongue meets the tip of him, I get a hint of salt and musk. And when I close my lips around the head, he's heavy on my tongue...

6. There is nothing sexier than the man who's begun to fuck my mouth in slow strokes because he just can't help himself.

7. Gag reflexes are real. When I'm a little too eager to please, my eyes start to water. Tom's hand eases up on my hair immediately, and his hips go still. I ease back and regain my equilibrium. And that hand slides kindly over my hair, waiting patiently for me.

8. When I begin to suck him again, he makes noises like the world is ending. I look up to watch, and the look of pleasure on his face just slays me. My eyes are still watering, but my goddamn emotions might have something to do with it.

9. Svenka wouldn't let emotions get in the way of hotel sex.

10. I'm not Svenka.

"Lie back, honeybunch." Tom's voice is rough as he nudges me onto the bed. But his words are gentle.

I add number eleven to my mental list of truths. *It's possible for sex to be rough and gentle at the same time.*

That is so confusing. I feel almost dizzy as I make myself more comfortable on the mattress. Meanwhile, he kicks off his trousers and hastily casts aside the rest of his clothing.

He is beautiful.

I'm not worthy.

This famous naked man climbs onto the bed with me. He gives me a boyish smile as he tugs the tie of my wrap dress open. "Holy. Fuck," he says. There is awe in his voice as my dress pools around me. It's his first glimpse of my new lingerie, which is made entirely of lengths of ribbon. "How did you—"

"—get this on? I tied one end to a doorknob and spun."

His eyes crinkle in the corners when he smiles. And then his eyes merge together like a cyclops.

Okay, not really. It's just that he's leaned down to kiss me again, and I can't focus on both of them at once. And my brain is melting, because the kisses are so good. I wrap my arms around this naked hunk of a man and hold him close. These kisses are different. Or maybe I'm different. I know him better now. And I know him better than the women who watch him on TV. I'm wearing his ring, for fuck's sake.

Fun hotel sex, I remind myself. And it is. But when he groans into the next kiss, the sound of his desire resonates inside me. I can feel the scruff of his not-quite-a-beard on my neck, my chin. I want to feel that scruff between my legs.

"Mmm," he says. "Sounds like a plan."

Apparently I said that out loud.

"But, fuck, honey. How do I get this thing off you?"

"Um..." I didn't think it would be complicated.

Tom's handy fingers get to work, loosening the parts at my hips and wriggling the straps off my shoulders. He unwraps me, throwing ribbon everywhere. It's looped over his body and under mine. We probably look like a bit of performance art gone wrong, but I don't much care. Because then his mouth is on me. His tongue is... Wow. A place tongues have never gone before. I move my hips, pushing up towards him because I want more of this. He makes me feel so filthy.

So alive.

And it's not Svenka who's fucking Tom's face, it's me. I'm not afraid to moan and writhe and let him know how hot and naughty he makes me feel.

"Now!" I order him. "You!" I'm about as articulate as Tarzan, but somehow he knows I need that cock, and I need it right fucking now.

He finds the condom beneath the ribbon debris and pushes that big body up on one arm. He rips the condom open with his teeth, and I help him roll it on. I so don't want to use a condom right now. I'd rather have his velvety skin inside me. But reason wins out.

Besides, rolling the condom on him is hot.

I lie back down on the bed, my lower legs hanging over the edge. I'm too greedy to position myself more carefully. And he doesn't care.

He leans right over and guides himself to me. I watch as he slides inside on a groan.

"Wait," he rasps. Then he puts his forearms on the bed (those forearms! I watched them hold a power drill!) He grabs a length of ribbon and gives a twist until we're bound, arm to arm. Tied together. I'm completely at his mercy.

And holy shit. Can this man use his tools or what?

Then he begins to thrust as we're literally tied to one another, and it's... There aren't words for this.

His body is ungodly. Or maybe godly. Maybe just plain holy. Like holy hell. His chest muscles flex with each push. He moans a bit and bites his bottom lip and I can't help but push back against him. The bed bounces beneath me with the power of his big body thrusting against mine.

And that's all she wrote. Everything goes golden, and I shudder. Then he groans and I can feel him pulse inside me. The sound he makes brings out something primal in me. For a brief second, I can imagine my life like this beyond the space-aged hotel room. At home in my house. His house. The various patios and porches...

But then I force myself to stop. I'm not thinking long term with Tom. I can't. I need to be in the now. This, after all, is just fucking.

"Holy shit," he says.

He's still inside me, softening a bit, but I love this quiet moment of still being joined.

"I agree," I say.

And then after another moment, he pulls out, and collapses next to me. We're both breathing hard and full of endorphins. No wonder people take drugs. I know exactly the high they're chasing.

It's all good until we realize we're still tied up in the ribbons.

Let me be clearer. Tom is such a fucking master with knots, that he's somehow tangled us together and we are, for lack of a better term, completely stuck.

"Fuck," he says.

I yank on my arm and his big hand moves, as if he's waving at me. He's my marionette. And I'm his.

There are two ways I could go here. I could freak the fuck out, or I could make his hand wave at me and dissolve into laughter.

Let me tell you, dissolving is even better than being untied.

Tom

It takes us a while to figure how to get untangled, and it's more than a little awkward. Somehow we manage, and I take her into the shower and rub my hands all over her.

It takes a while.

Eventually we're free. And hungry. All that nakedness has our appetites worked up.

Our? Fuck. I'm starting to talk like we're really a couple. Like a permanent couple.

That's not cool.

Still. "Can't we just stay here forever?" I ask her as she's getting ready for dinner. She's got the bathroom door open, and I get a glimpse of a naked leg slipping into something, an arm being draped.

I'm joking about staying here forever, but not really. I'd be just as happy ordering in and feasting off her for the rest of the night. Hell, the rest of the year. Brynn or Svenka, or whoever she wants to be, turns me into a teenager with a constant erection and an inability to keep my paws off her.

I think I deserve a little of the credit here, my dick says.

"We *could* stay here forever," she says as she leans towards the bathroom mirror and smooths some lipstick over her plump mouth. I want to lick her. "But if we were here forever then that couch would definitely have to go." She air-kisses her reflection, and I just stand there watching her with a big old smile on my face.

Chandra never let me see her put on makeup. She never let me see her without makeup, either. She was always perfect in a way that was a little unsettling. And, as sexy as it is undressing someone, watching Brynn get dressed is actually equally exciting, maybe even a little more, because I know later tonight I'm going to be taking it all off again. Slowly. Piece by piece.

"What are you hungry for?" I ask. "Publicist Becky made us five different reservations. There's a list on my phone. You can choose..." I find the email and rattle off five different restaurant names.

"Yes," she says.

"Yes?"

"I want all the food. Just...all of it. You'd better choose. I have analysis paralysis. Choose anything you want as long as it will look pretty in a picture. I need shots for my blog."

Her blog. I'd forgotten about that. "So the gourmet porridge place is out?"

Brynn's pretty face appears in the doorway. "The...what?"

"Kidding! Gullible much?"

She sticks out her tongue and disappears into the bathroom again.

Laughing, I scroll through the list of restaurants again. If she were Chandra, she wouldn't actually eat the food, she'd just want it to look perfect. But Brynn...this is a woman with an appetite to match mine.

So I know just the place.

31 POPPIN' SOME BALLS

Brynn

The restaurant Tom chose is amazing. Although I'm distracted by the waiter's silky black shirt. It's unbuttoned halfway to his navel. That seems to be the style at this restaurant. My sexual appetite has clearly spun into overdrive, because all that coppery skin makes it challenging to focus on the man's words. But I buckle down and concentrate, because he's explaining something important.

"...you flip the coaster to the green side when you're ready to be served. And don't flip it back to the red side until you can't eat another thing."

I have to swallow because my mouth is already watering from the scent of Brazilian barbecue in the air. "What's your favorite meat?" I ask, and then stifle a giggle. Because it's clear that the waiters serving the beefsteak are all beefcake.

"Well, the sirloin rocks," our young, unbuttoned waiter assures us. "But you also don't want to miss the pork tenderloin. It's marinated in lime, garlic, and soy sauce. So save room for that."

"Good tip," I say, getting hungrier by the second.

"I'll get those caipirinhas right out to you. In the meantime, help yourself to the appetizer bar." He points to a ridiculously long buffet in the middle of the room. "And enjoy!"

Tom lets out a happy sigh. "You heard the man. Let's do this."

I follow him toward the appetizers, and he hands me a plate. "Brynn—this is very important — these right here are the key to life." He uses tongs to transfer four little golden balls to my plate.

"I love balls," I say, and I draw out the word *balls*. Because I am a teenager.

We load up our plates, then gallop back to the table, where I try the little ball-shaped fritters right away. "Oh. My. God." I'm having a cheese orgasm. A *cheesegasm*. "What was that?"

"I know, right? They call it a pão de queijo."

I eat another one immediately. Each one is a savory puff of pastry, filled with salty cheese. "Where have these been all my life? I'm going to make some when we get home." I just have to. It's hard to take a minute and snap some pictures for reference, but I force myself to, because I feel like I've stumbled onto a eureka moment here. Baaaaallllllls.

"My kitchen is available," Tom says with a wink. "I'll be your taste tester."

I give him a big smile, and it takes me a long beat to remember that cooking to please men isn't something I want to do anymore. But Tom makes it easy to forget. He looks at me with hungry eyes—but not for food.

That would probably change if we were a real couple. He'd get sick of me just like Steve did. When he looked at me a year from now, he'd only see the dinner plate in my hands.

Nope. Not going there again. I am a new woman, or at least a slightly improved, more focused woman.

We mow down our appetizers in companionable silence. It's comfortable, this quiet. Not like when you're on a first date and you feel like you're about to be prepped for a pap smear. This is the kind of quiet where there's no spike and anxiety and the only clenching of thighs is because I'm excited, not panicked. Then Tom taps my red coaster. "Ready?"

"Bring it on."

He smiles at me and then flips the coaster to the green side. Ten seconds later two glorious things happen: our unbuttoned waiter sets two minty, frothy drinks on the table. And *another* half-clad waiter pauses beside me, hoisting a two-foot metal barbecue spit over my plate. I swear to god there's a fan pointed at him because his hair is blowing like he's an old-school romance cover model. It makes me want to spritz him. With something. Lost my focus. Oh! Food. There are several pounds of luscious, browned pork impaled on the metal spike. "Ham?" the young man asks.

"Don't mind if we do!" Tom says.

The man uses a scary-looking knife to shave a healthy slice of meat off the spit, then deftly angles it to fall right on my plate. Then he does the same for Tom.

"Wow." I cut off a corner of the meat and tuck it into my mouth. "This is amazing. Let's just move in here and call it good."

"You are seriously fun," Tom says, popping another cheese ball into his mouth. "My ex would only eat protein shakes and kale juice."

"Sounds like a party." Then I grimace, and it's only partly because of kale juice. *Do not ask about his ex*, I coach myself. *You do not want to know*. Tonight is not for reality. Tonight is for dining on Brazilian barbecue in a big restaurant full of half-dressed waiters who parade ten different kinds of meat around the room.

Tonight is pretty damn good.

"Does my favorite foodie want a glass of red wine to go with her dinner?" Tom asks. "Or should we stick with the caipirinhas?"

"That is a seriously tough choice." I give it some thought. "Let's stick with the caipirinhas, because we can have red wine anytime." Although—hang on—the taste of my drink makes me wonder if my blog should branch out to exotic cocktails too. But the ingredients might be a challenge. "They must buy mint by the bushel here."

Tom shrugs. "Mint is the easiest thing in the world to grow—it'll take over the garden if you let it. So will oregano. That whole family of herbs are bullies in the garden. You can't kill 'em even if you try."

"Really?" I want that—wonderful herbs outside my back door. "I think I need an herb garden, then. I want to waltz right outside and pluck mint and oregano for my recipes. And sprigs of herbs would look great in my blog photographs."

"You know what's funny?" Tom asks, waving down a waiter who's carrying a giant skewer of steak. "You and I are in the same line of work almost. I make houses pretty, and you make pretty food."

I snort. "The difference is that you're successful at it."

"We'll see." His face darkens.

"Wait. Didn't it go well today?" Now I feel like a heel for not

SARINA BOWEN & TANYA EBY

asking sooner. I'd leapt on him the second he came home. There had been no time to ask.

Tom fiddles with his fork. "The network is being difficult about..."

"Our video?"

"Yeah. They're waiting to see how their conservative viewers will react, which pisses me off. Like—just decide for yourself, you cowards. If they fired me, I could get mad and move on. But now I'm in the awkward place of trying to prove that I'm worthy." He rolls his eyes. "I hate it."

"Oh, honey!" I cover his hand with mine. "I'm so sorry. Those turds. They'd be crazy to fire you. I mean, I'm no expert, but you have a really fine way of holding your, ehm, hammer."

He gives me a soft smile. "That is very nice of you to say, especially since you'd never heard of my show until we met."

Whoops. I was not about to confess that I'd gotten all turned on binge-watching it today. "I'm a very loyal fake fiancé."

"You are." His smile warms, and he strokes my hand with his big Man Thumb. And that Man Thumb makes me all quivery. Throbby. That's not a pretty word, but by god, it's the truth.

From my handbag comes a ring tone loud enough to be heard over the crowded restaurant. *Classy.* I grab the phone and silence it.

"Anything important?" Tom asks.

"That's just my mother calling." I roll my eyes. "Definitely not a good reason to interrupt this feast we're having."

"Shit." Tom sits back in his chair. "Is your mother having a hard time with..."

"Her daughter's porn career?" I shrug. "Honestly, I think she can't decide whether she's embarrassed, or whether she's enjoying the extra attention the other retirees are giving her."

My mother *had* chewed me out for showing the world my sex face. But in her next breath she'd admitted that she'd been invited to four extra bridge parties and that every speck of her tuna casserole had been eaten at the Sunday potluck.

She stopped short of thanking me, though.

I grab my phone out of my bag and show him the text.

Mom: I've been thinking since seeing that video,

you might want to try a body buff to take care of dead skin. These things matter more as you get older.

"See?" I say. "Clearly not a big deal. She's not too traumatized to remind me that I'm getting older. Let's just hope the universities feel the same way. That they're more concerned about exfoliation than the morality of their potential writing professor."

Tom puts a big hand over his face. "I'm so sorry. The job thing is bad enough, but it never occurred to me that I'd embarrassed you to your family."

It hits me that he's said something a little odd. "Don't you have a family to embarrass?"

"Nope." He stabs his fork into the barbecued beef that's just landed on our plates.

This is puzzling. "Everybody has some family, right?"

"Not everybody." His face shuts down, and it's obvious that he doesn't want to talk about it.

I don't even know why I push. "Are you estranged? Or are they gone?"

"Gone," he murmurs, and doesn't look me in the eye.

"Oh." I'm stunned. There's something so warm and easygoing about Tom, and I would have bet cash money that he'd grown up in a big, loud family. I don't know what to say. So I cover one of his hands with my free one.

My other hand is busy shoveling food into my mouth. The marinated pork tenderloin shows up, and it's amazing. As are the grilled prawns. And the grilled salmon. And more steak. We eat until I'm sure were going to burst. I don't press on the family thing. I can tell it's a sensitive spot, and I'm not sure we're ready yet for those tender places.

An hour later we stumble out onto the sidewalk. My wrap dress is tight. So naturally someone shoves a camera in our faces. The flash blinds me.

"Hey! It's Mr. Fixit Quick! Can I have a selfie?"

"Um, sure," he says. "But just quick, because my fiancée is waiting for me."

There's a shrill, female squeal. And when my eyes start working again, I spot two tourists posing with Tom, who looks annoyed even through his I'm-posing-for-a-photo smile.

"When's the wedding?" the woman asks.

Tom's gaze meets mine, and we realize at once that we haven't worked out that part of our story yet.

"It's top secret!" I say quickly. "We don't want wedding crashers. But we're going with an exotic cocktails theme," I babble. "Mai tais and caipirinhas. Drinks with lime! And, uh, citrus-colored bridesmaids dresses."

"I thought you said seafoam," Tom argues. Then he winks at me.

"*Honey*," I protest, one hand on my hip. "Seafoam is so 2012. That's why I picked lime and tangelo."

"Oh, right. Tangelo." His eyes crinkle in the corners, and I can't wait to get him into bed again.

32 A KISS. A SQUEEZE. A BURP.

Brynn

The very next day there's a story on *BuzzPop* proclaiming citrus colors—including tangelo—as the new big thing in bridal wear.

Also, Tom surprises me with tickets to *Hamilton*. I think I pee myself a little with excitement. "How did you DO that?" I squeal, clinging to him.

"I made a call, and my agent scared up a couple seats to the matinee. And the show is a couple years old now. Not quite as hot as the color tangelo."

We giggle all the way there, and then we both pretend not to cry at the sad ending.

It's the perfect trip. Perfect. But then it's over, and I find myself blinking up at the sign for LaGuardia airport and wondering how my trip—and my escape from real life—could reach such a sudden end. As I take my seat in first class on the jet, it hits me that I haven't planned beyond this point.

The stewardess asks for Tom's autograph and coos over my fake-engagement ring—the one that I've gotten used to seeing on my hand. "When's the wedding?" she asks.

"Top secret," we both reply. But it isn't as funny today for some reason.

It's not even three hours later when he drops me off at home. "Your bag is heavy, I can..." He starts to get out of the truck.

"I've got it! I need the exercise!" I don't want him to come inside with me, because I've just spent a lot of quality time pretending that he's mine. And it's begun to confuse me.

But he catches my hand in his before I can leap out of the truck. "Hey." His voice is low and growly, and I shiver, because I now know exactly how that voice sounds against my ear while he's inside me. "I have to kiss my fiancée goodbye."

Oh. "Someone might be watching."

Slowly, he nods. But his eyes are on mine, and I'm not sure either one of us really believes that other people exist. Not right this moment. He leans in, and his lips are softer and gentler than they've been before. I sigh into his kiss, and his Man Hands run down my back one last time.

Wow.

"That looks wobbly," he says, and I assume he's talking about my knees after that kiss.

"I'll pull myself together." Then I notice he's pointing at the railing on my little porch stoop. "Oh, it's been like that since I moved in. I'm careful."

"Hmm. That's going to bug me. It's not safe." He chews his lip. "You know, your fiancé wouldn't just let that go. He'd probably fix that crack in your kitchen floor too."

"In the first place, it's a rental," I point out. "And in the second place, you and a real fiancée wouldn't bother with this house. We'd move into your mansion on the lake." *Duh.*

"No we wouldn't." Tom makes a face. "Not there."

This makes me gasp. "Don't you like it? It's beautiful."

"It's okay." He avoids my gaze by looking past me at my rental. "This could be a cute little Victorian if someone gave it some care."

"I suppose. But I have other things on my mind."

Like *you.*

He kisses me again or I kiss him and then we part, letting our hands slowly drift apart as violins swell and the scene fades to gray then black.

Sorry. I got a little melodramatic there. Actually, he kisses me, squeezes my ass and says "I'll call ya."

"Okay," I say and then hold in a burp. Because that's real-life romance.

33 FUCKING LA LA LAND

Tom

It's late in the afternoon and I'm sitting in my office waiting for Patricia to Skype me. She's trying to stay on top of technology, and it's painful for both of us. When I shut my eyes, I'm back in the thick of New York. Exhaust. Noise. Honking horns. Neon even in the middle of the day. People pissed off and being super verbal about why they're pissed off. My business trips to New York are sometimes fun, but I prefer the quiet of Michigan.

An image floats into my mind of a little lake cottage—not in the 'burbs like my mansion, but on the big lake—with a picture window. The front door is painted hunter green. There's a screened-in porch on one side...

The fantasy calms me enough that when Patricia finally comes online, I'm ready for her.

As much as she wants to be "modern," she really doesn't know what she's doing. "Hello? Tom? Tom are you fucking there?" She's hollering and I am staring at her very large chest where her buttons are holding on for dear life to keep her covered. It would only take one really deep inhale to send those buttons shooting across the room.

"I'm here, Patricia. You have to angle your screen up."

"WHAT?"

"Adjust your monitor. Up. No, not like...yes! Stop! There you go."

"Oh," she says and then she sits down, so now I can only see her face from the eyes up. Her shaggy, dark eyebrows (Benjamin Moore's Ashwood Moss) are very expressive though, so it's fine.

"I have just offered you a very nice deal and your mind is off in fucking la la land."

"Um, what are you talking about? I don't have an offer from you."

"I emailed it to you." There's a pause. "Oh. Fuck." Then I hear clicking. And said email appears in my inbox. "Look, the network has an idea, and I think it's genius. This is your chance to prove to them that your thrusting butt cheeks aren't a big deal."

Closing my eyes, I have to picture the cottage again to stay calm. *Hunter green door. Beach sand on the front porch.* Patricia and I have known each other a long time, but I'd hoped we could go another ten years without having a conversation about my bare ass.

"You've had a nice, comfy hiatus, Tom. But it's time for you to get back to work. And by back to work, I mean you need to leave that shithole town in Michigan and go rescue some historic homes!"

Patricia doesn't get paid unless I get paid, so it's natural that she'd want me back at work. And the idea of knocking down some walls sounds pretty good right now. What I really want to do is knock on Brynn's door. Maybe hold her up against a wall... Damn it. I'm doing it again. "So they gave the green light to season ten?"

The eyes take on a furtive look. "Not exactly. But they're going to. Right now they're offering you a nice, fat fee for a special. A fucking special! You'll only be on location for a week. And if that pans out, they'll hand you a contract for season ten."

"What kind of special? Please tell me it doesn't involve a musical number." If Patricia has booked me on *Dancing with the Stars*, I may not be responsible for my actions.

"A musical number?" she pauses. "Ah. That is a joke. I get it. Don't quit your day job. No. There's no music, hot buns. This is another Speed Build—a quick rescue and revamp of an old ski lodge. Here's the deal—your network's sister network needs to shoot a reality show there in two weeks' time. But somebody got their wires crossed, and they didn't renovate on schedule." She cackles, then waves a manicured hand past her eyes. "I don't know how a bunch of overpaid suits could make so many mistakes, honestly. But their dipshittedness is your gain. The network wants to fly you out immediately. You'll prep the site, make some plans, and renovate everything in a forty-eight-hour continuous roll."

It's weird, but I can feel my pulse jump. I love a challenge. And I'd forgotten how it feels to be given a mission.

"If the special succeeds, they're actually prepared to offer you a five-season renewal. It's unheard of, really."

Five years? That's a long time.

Wow.

"Wow," I say, trying to remain enthusiastic. "But what if the special tanks, and it's not my fault? What if they put me up against a boxing match on cable? Are you telling me my whole career is hanging on this special?"

"It's going to be fine," she insists. "This opportunity is golden. Also, I want a trip to Italy with my grandchildren, so you are going to sign this contract and hop on a plane to renovate a ski house. Come on, hot buns. Opportunity calls!"

I'm trying to process all of this. And trying to rein in my desire to argue about 1) the horrible new nickname she's given me, and 2) the fact that nobody really faxes anymore. "A ski house, huh?" I ask instead. "Where did you say it was?"

I'm afraid of her answer. I really am. But couldn't it be in Michigan? Couldn't reality stars do their thing in a lake cottage? That way Brynn and I could kick back with a glass of wine and some of her balls that's she's working on and, I don't know, watch the sunset?

But that's not the answer I get from Patricia. Patricia is a beast. She eats the Easter Bunny for breakfast. Raw. With her bare hands.

"It's in Quebec," she says. "That's in Canada, in case you're curious."

Something kicks me in the gut. I'm pretty sure it's Patricia's boot. I can't speak, really, so I check the email with the contract.

I look at the amount offered. Flip through the terms.

"I'm telling you, Tom, if you don't agree to this, then they're going to lose patience. You get that, right? You've had this show forever, and there is new blood out there, and I don't like to be the bearer of bad news, but timing matters. The network needs your help on this. This is your chance to remind them you belong on that network."

Who am I kidding? Of course I'm going to do the special. I don't want to give up my career just because the network is being prudish. And if it's a success, this might help out Brynn. Her fake fiancé's career comeback could help hers along too.

And anyway—what else am I going to do? Stay here in Michigan? Hide away in my big empty house? Dream up a cozy little cottage? Ask Brynn to move in with me?

Now there's a ridiculous idea. She wouldn't want me for keeps. Sure the sex is great, but she doesn't know the real me. It's not like I'm relationship material. I'm just a man with big hands and a...hammer.

Fuck it. I need this distraction. And even if I don't sign on for season ten, I can walk away from it all with my head held high.

Even better—maybe the whole "special" thing could take the spotlight off Brynn so she can get on with her life.

That's the thing that pushes me to decide.

"When do we start?" I ask.

34 BRAZILIAN CHEESE PUFFS CAN FIX EVERYTHING EXCEPT HEARTACHE

Brynn

After we return from New York, I get busy planning my future. I don't have a color-coded weekly planner like Ash does, but that doesn't matter. I send out another batch of résumés, and I research how to legally change my name. I'm going to give the job search three months, and if it doesn't work, drastic measures will be called for.

And then? I wait.

Waiting sucks.

A lot.

But I refuse to become a basket case. So I reward myself for this burst of productivity in two ways. First, I find a recipe for pão de queijo. It calls for tapioca flour, and because that's a carb—and because I'm me—I have some already.

Second, I prop up my tablet on the kitchen counter and stream another episode of *Mr. Fixit Quick* while I work on the cheese-puff dough. In this one, Tom is renovating a barn in Montana. It's a big job to convert it into a house, but the red structure is adorable. I'm ready to relocate to Montana the moment Tom installs a set of sliding glass doors which open up the home to mountain views.

But then there's a plot twist. And I'm not ready.

Tom is building a deck, which means I get to watch him use a nail gun. The flex of his biceps on each nail makes me a little crazy. There

I am in my happy place, stirring cheese into dough and watching my favorite guy *nail things* (rawr!), when he decides he needs to admire the view, just to make sure they've set up the deck correctly.

"Quality control," he says to the camera with a smile.

There's a time lapse of the sun beginning to set and glow orange. Tom stands at the deck railing, facing that gorgeous sunset. And that's when Chandra the decorator carries two glasses of champagne onto the deck, handing one to my man.

And then? She snuggles up to his side and he puts his arm around her, *pulling her closer.*

I let out a little shriek of dismay. Of course the camera lingers on them—two gorgeous people together in a gorgeous place. But I can't take it. I need to stop the video. My hands are sticky with butter and dough, so I lean over and touch pause with my nose. As one does.

Fucking Chandra. No, really. He is *fucking Chandra?* She's his ex? Seriously?

My happy place is less happy than it was a few minutes ago, in spite of being coated with butter and cheese. I plop balls of dough onto a cookie sheet, trying to decide what this means. He's never said Chandra's name before. But you don't snuggle your coworker unless you're sleeping with her.

Who am I kidding? He probably sleeps with hordes of women. A gorgeous man working in television could pick up a different girl at every Home Depot in America.

And why do I care so much?

When the cheese puffs are in the oven, and the timer is set, I wash my hands and check the video again, in case my hormones got the best of me, and the scene isn't exactly as I'd first thought.

Nope. When I rewind, it actually gets worse. Because this time I'm ready, and I get a good look at the macho way he tucks her into his side. I swear he did the same thing with me just two nights ago, as we walked up Seventh Avenue.

And I freaking loved it.

Fuck.

I check the timer, because it's obvious that eating a dozen or so cheese puffs is the only thing that will make me feel better. Wait—there's something else. I text Sadie and Ash.

> *Me: Does anyone want to discuss thirty seconds of*
> *video and cheer me up? Where are you guys?*
> *Ash: Working on a listing.*
> *Sadie: Busy cleaning the girls' bedroom. Sorry!*
> *Me: I have Brazilian cheese puffs and wine.*
> *They're still warm. (The cheese puffs, not*
> *the wine.)*
> *Ash: I'll be there in five.*
> *Sadie: Don't eat them all without me!*

"I'm sorry, honey. But that was definitely a cuddle," Ash says pragmatically.

"Although I didn't see a butt grab," Sadie points out.

"Maybe you can't grab butts in prime time," I venture.

"Let's Google her," Ash says, reaching for her phone.

"No!" I yell. "Don't. Really. I don't want to know. She looks five years younger than me, and forty pounds lighter." Plus, Tom and I once agreed not to Google each other.

Ash puts her phone away without a word and then tops up my glass of wine.

Just after we've eaten the last of the balls, my phone rings. And when I see that it's Tom, I get a crazy little smile on my face. I know this because Ash and Sadie point and laugh.

"Hush, bitches," I insist as I answer. "Hello?"

"Hi," he says, his voice a low scrape.

I feel tingles just from that one word. "Hiiiii," I sigh into the phone, while Ash and Sadie clap their hands over their mouths to keep from laughing at me. I march into the kitchen for a little privacy.

"I have news. I wanted to tell them in person, but it looks like I'm jumping on a flight tonight."

"Them?" I ask, confused.

"You," he says quickly. "And your boobs. I was just thinking about your boobs. Sorry."

"No problem," I say. Now my nipples are tingling. And then I realize that he just said he was flying away. "Where are you going?"

"Quebec. The network wants me to shoot a special."

"That's great!" I say, even though I really don't mean it. I thought we had a few more weeks to be fake-engaged together. I was really looking forward to it.

"It's all right," he says. "Not quite as good as being naked with you."

Now my *everything* is tingling. "It's a good sign that the network wants you back, though." That had been the point of our fake engagement, anyway. Is he done with me so soon?

"We'll see," he says. "They're in a bind, and this is my chance to help them out. The pay is pretty great too. We'll have to celebrate when I get back in a couple of weeks."

"I'd love to celebrate with you." Anytime. Anyhow. I've got it bad.

"Is that right?" His voice gets all low and sexy. "How do you think we should celebrate?"

"Chocolate and sex," I whisper.

"Mmm," he groans into my ear. "I'll bring truffles and my dick."

We both giggle. But when my laughter dies out, I'm craving him, and he's still getting on a plane.

Damn it.

"Take care of yourself," I tell him.

"You too," he whispers.

We hang up, and he heads off to pack for Quebec.

I have to make another batch of Brazilian balls just to cheer myself up.

35 WEAVE YOUR MAGIC

Tom

On the plane to Quebec, I'm full of enthusiasm. It feels great to get back to work, and I can't wait to see my team. Note to self—brooding alone at home for several months was bad for the soul. Brynn had made it all better, of course.

Only my relationship with her wasn't real.

My job, on the other hand, is very real. I rent a Land Rover at the airport in Montreal and drive into the mountains. When I stop at a McDonald's, everyone speaks only French. I buy a "hamburger avec fromage" and it tastes better than usual because I ordered it in a different language.

Now, a guy could get seriously spoiled by Brynn's cooking. But I have to put that right out of my mind, because this is my life—a different rental truck in every town. Fast food on the way to the site. Teasing Larry, my master electrician, about his facial hair.

I can do this. No fear.

It helps that when I roll up to the old ski resort they want me to renovate, it's beautiful. The long lodge is nestled into a stand of pines. There're two big stone fireplaces, one at either end of the structure. I like this building immediately. It has gravitas.

When I go inside, I can already see what needs to be done. The rooms are dark because the lower level has been chopped into too many rooms. I'm going to open it up to let the space breathe. Changing the envelope of the house would take too long, but I can enlarge a few crucial windows and still meet my deadline.

"Hey, Burt!" I yell to my carpentry assistant who's already measuring the grand staircase. "Get over here! Let's talk window framing."

"Dude!" The younger man gallops toward me and then wraps me in a big, back-slapping man hug. "That's the greeting I get? I've missed your big grumpy self. And now I need details about this fiancée of yours. Way to break the internet, dude. A sex tape? It's always the quiet ones." He's grinning like a Jack-o'-lantern.

"We will not be discussing that," I growl.

"Sure thing, hot buns." He cracks up.

"Have you been talking to Patricia?"

"Maybe!" He giggles. "Seriously, though. Where is this girl? I have to meet the one who said yes instead of no."

She didn't, though. It's not real. "She's in Michigan. Working," I mumble. Until this second, the lie hasn't been much of a hardship. I don't have any family to let down when Brynn and I "break up." But I like Burt and the other guys on my crew. I could confide in them, but then things would get messy. And, anyway, the lie will be over soon enough.

Down the road, when Burt consoles me with beer over my new breakup—the way he did when Chandra let me down—it won't even be hard to act sad.

In the meantime, I have a lodge to renovate. "Does this place need our help, or what?" I say, looking around. "This is going to be very gratifying."

"I know, right? It's time to weave your magic, boss man. Right now it gives off a moldering dump vibe. But you'll bring the sparkledust. By the time we're done, I'll never want to leave."

That's the goal, and I'm good at my job. Just over a week from now there'll be honeyed rays of sunlight streaming in this room, where now there's only dimness. A picture window with comfortable furniture. I can tell that two or three of the pines outside will have to go. The trees are great, but the people who live here—or stay here a while, because this is for some kind of reality show—will sit down on the sofa and cast their gazes at the mountains out the window. They'll linger in this room and feel happy.

I'll make sure of it.

Twenty-four hours later, I'm singing a different tune. Honestly, *Dancing with the Stars* might actually be easier than finishing this job.

It's not Quebec's fault. It's really fucking beautiful here, but now that only pisses me off. The rugged mountains and the piney scent ought to make me happy. But they don't, because the network wants me to do the unthinkable: a tacky renovation.

In all my years in TV, I've never had creative differences with the network. They don't usually care what I do as long as the owner cries tears of joy when I'm done. But this time it's different, because the homeowner is the producer of one of those shows where seventeen scandals happen before the first commercial break.

No wonder the pay was so high. I didn't realize I would have to sell my soul to finish this project.

"You want glitz and shiny surfaces," I'm saying to the producer on our second day of pre-production. "But this old ski lodge you've chosen clearly demands a rustic, manly touch. There ought to be deer antlers on the wall, and rough-hewn beams."

He taps one shiny shoe on the floor and makes a *tsk-tsk* sound. "I need skylights in the den and a hot tub that seats sixteen."

"Sixteen?" I bark. "That's not a hot tub. That's a Roman orgy!"

"Have you even watched *Betrothed?*" the producer asks. "Orgies are not out of the question. Six engaged couples spend a month together to be sure their bonds are strong enough for marriage. It's a great vacation. But temptation is everywhere."

"Wait." My poor brain tries to wrap itself around this horrible concept. "So you put them all in bathing suits in a hot tub and see who cheats first?"

"The bathing suits are optional," he says with a snicker. His teeth are so white and shiny that I'm practically blinded.

I groan, when I'd really rather vomit.

"Now talk me through the upstairs renovation," he says. "How many skylights can I have?"

None, you fucker. "Skylights are a terrible idea in this climate. They'll cause ice damming in the winter, and the roof will leak."

Shiny Shoes gives a shrug. "I'll be long gone by then. And I need a lot of light fixtures everywhere, so we can capture the infidelities in HD."

Seriously, I want to bonk him over the head with my socket wrench. "I'll make sure the electrician is up to speed."

"The kitchen table has to sit at least a dozen people at once. No, wait—it needs to be the kind that can be either large or small depending on the need. As the couples break up and leave the show, I'll need a more intimate setting."

Gross. But the table is not my problem. "When the designer turns up, you can tell him all about it." Theoretically they're sending an interior designer tomorrow. And it's a damn good thing, because if Shiny Shoes wants mirrors on the ceiling, or heart-shaped beds, it's not my funeral.

I already heard him say something about a lilac color scheme. *Gag.*

My phone rings, and it's a thrilling sound, because it means I can escape from this fuckwit. "Excuse me," I say loudly, for the benefit of anyone in earshot. "My fiancée is on the line." Becky the publicist has asked me to refer to Brynn that way as often as possible.

And Brynn is making that easy for me, because it really is her on the phone. Eagerly, I step away from Shiny Shoes and move outdoors, where everything is calm and beautiful. "Hi, gorgeous," I answer.

"Hi!" she returns, sounding breathless. "I didn't get your text until now. I was kneading some dough."

"*Were* you now?" I say, dropping my voice. But I realize too late that "kneading some dough" doesn't sound the least bit sexy, so now I'm snorting and laughing and Brynn is giggling in my ear.

"I don't even want to know," she says, tittering.

Titters is such an awesome word. And just like that I feel all the frustrations of this job fall away. Ten seconds on the phone with Brynn is all it takes.

"I had some good news today," she says. "I'm making a loaf of cinnamon raisin bread to celebrate."

"Oh, wow. Cinnamon raisin bread is really good for toast. With butter…" My stomach rumbles.

"Don't you want to hear the news?"

"Of course. What happened?"

"I got an interview!" she cries.

"Congratulations! Where?" This *is* good news. Maybe I haven't ruined her life, after all.

"That little art college downtown—I almost didn't send my résumé. It's such a small school! But they called me this morning." The words get muffled. She's chewing on something.

"Are you cooking something besides the bread?"

"Am I breathing? Of course I am. Woman cannot dine on bread alone. She also needs bacon and poached eggs."

My stomach rumbles even though I ate only an hour ago. "Sure wish I could join you."

"Of course you do," she says cheerfully. "The bacon was hand-smoked by the guy at the farmers' market."

That's not the real reason I wish I was there, though. I can picture standing with Brynn in her shabby kitchen, and the image is so much more appealing than the one I've got in front of me here. A week from now I'll have rebuilt this place with a gleaming, chef's gourmet kitchen. And I don't even care.

Fuck.

"The network is pissing me off." I sigh into the phone. "I wish I was at home with you."

There's a silence on the line while Brynn absorbs this bit of truth. What I want her to say is, *Then come home*.

"What did they do?" she asks instead.

"This project is sleazy," I complain. Because it is. "I worry that they're trying to position me in a different, sleazier way than they used to. As if showing the world my ass has changed my image, so they're just going to drive me like an out-of-control belt sander until I crash into something."

"I'm sorry," she says sweetly.

Aw. "It's okay. I'll be fine. I just have to remember why I got into the business—to build spaces for happy families."

"That's an excellent reason," she assures me. "Everyone deserves a nice home."

I'm embarrassed now, so I mutter something about being good with my hands. But it's been a while since I stated my purpose out loud. And it occurs to me that part of the reason I've been building family homes for almost twenty years is that I never had one for myself.

Last year I *tried* to make a home for myself, but I went about it the wrong way, and it flopped.

Must have built it for the wrong girl.

This epiphany is interrupted by my pal, Burt, who's waving to me with both hands. That probably means that Shiny Shoes has just found a new way to wreck the project, and that I'd better go do some more damage control.

"I gotta go," I tell Brynn reluctantly.

"Are you okay?" she asks.

"Yeah," I say quickly. That's what a man is supposed to say. "Talk soon?"

"Of course."

I love you. The words are on the tip of my tongue, and they almost tumble out. Except that's not how Brynn and I are with each other, and nobody is listening so I can't even claim it as an act of publicity. "Take care of yourself," I say instead.

There's a pause and then she says, "You too!"

We hang up, and I spend the next half hour verbally wrestling with every idea that comes out of Shiny Shoes's mouth.

I like to create spaces where happy family lives are meant to be lived. He wants a space where great drama happens. The two goals are incompatible. In order to rein in my fury, I stop listening. Instead, I just watch his mouth move while nodding occasionally.

But one thing is clear. I need to stop brooding over my personal life and pay more attention to my career before everything goes to shit. Some people aren't meant to get a Happily Ever After, and that's just the way it is.

36 IT AIN'T EASY BEING PINK

Brynn

After I talk to Tom, my heart hurts. I don't understand it. So I try to be upbeat. I try to be enthusiastic, and I think I pull it off.

I'm so confused.

I blame my mom.

No, for real. When I called him I'd just survived my weekly visit with her. My mom is a consummate up-grader. She's been married four times and is looking for number five. She reads self-help books for fun. And she can't be bothered with cooking, so it's all take out and instant just-add-water dishes for her. I think she's also why I cook so much. When you're raised on TV dinners and chipped-beef on toast because it's all your mom can throw together before heading out on another date, there's something really comforting about a home-cooked meal.

Whatever. I digress.

She means well, she does. Which is why she came over to give me a pep talk. She walked in, kissed my cheek, and immediately started unpacking the grocery bags from cleaning out her cupboards. Now I have a stack of instant gravy mix, Kraft macaroni and cheese, and Chicken NoodleO's. Not even the contestants on *Chopped* could come up with something edible from that.

And while she unpacked and rearranged my cupboards, which I

will rearrange back, she shared with me this nugget of mom wisdom: I'm too emotional. "Maybe that's why you couldn't hold Steve's interest. You're so glum all the time. No man wants to be tied to a woman whose aura is gray. You need to be leopard-spotted. Or at least a color. Try being pink!"

After that, I sort of zoned out, but damn it if her words didn't seep into my brain a little.

When I spoke to Tom on the phone, I was trying very hard to be pink.

I fucking hate pink.

But sure! *Life is good! It's totally fine that you're in Quebec filming a swanky show! I'm happy here, unemployed, in my kitchen, rolling balls. I have a master's in English language and literature and I'm currently watching Turner Classic Movies in black and white because I am depressed.*

I guess pink just isn't my color.

Whenever I talk to Tom, though, I really do feel more colorful. I want to stay like that. I don't want to be a drain. I don't want to be an effort. So I talk in exclamation points! It's awkward and it hurts my mouth. And also my heart.

Shake it off, Brynn. It's for the best. (My mom also mentioned the power of self-talk.)

And I can.

I will.

I mean, I! Will!

But first, I'm going to polish off this bacon, and then actually take a shower. I have my interview at the art school this afternoon. The head of the department sounded panicked when she called, so maybe things are looking up for me.

For once, it's someone else panicking.

It takes about ten minutes to drive downtown from my place. The last time I was downtown was with Tom that awkward night at Tai One On and the paparazzi. It was also the night when we stealthily escaped across Reed's Lake. Maybe that was the moment I started falling for him. In the middle of the lake, surrounded by the quiet lapping of the water against the boat, watching Tom paddle by starlight.

And now I'm horny. Again. Still.

Focus, Brynn!

Maybe the self-talk is getting a little much. I'd much rather write a list. As I walk toward the glass building that houses the art college, I start to compose one in my head.

1) Get this job.

And that's as far as I get, because I open the front doors and step into a college building that's different from anything I've ever seen. I say that without an ounce of hyperbole, because to access the college offices, you first have to walk through an installation of a vagina. Literally. I'm walking through a vagina, and it's all warm and soft fabric, and there's a breeze blowing. I giggle a little because this is a really big vagina. The installation ends not with a wider exploration of the uterus, but at a normal-looking front desk.

Something tells me I'm going to like it here.

I'm whisked upstairs by the receptionist to meet with the head of curriculum development. Her name is Hazel and I want her to be my grandmother. She's petite, with fluffy white hair. She has reading glasses and wears a cardigan over a flowery dress. This is not a person you would expect to work at a place where the front door is a giant vagina. Except I notice a discreet tattoo peeking out from under the cuff of her cardigan. You just never know about people.

She smells of patchouli and I love her.

The interview goes like this. "Brynn. It's nice to meet you. You have ten years of teaching experience? Why did they fire you?"

No beating around the bush here. "I got divorced from the dean's son. They claimed budget cuts."

She snorts. "Fucking budget cuts. We have them too. Here's the deal. We need someone to take over four classes. Three sessions of freshman writing, and one on writing about art. The woman who was supposed to teach them was on sabbatical and fucking fell in love while on a cruise or something with a woman named Thora. They met in Iceland. I don't understand the story fully, but it involves a fjord and following her heart. Anyway. She's quit. Up and quit! And we are, to use a cliché, forgive me, up shit's creek without a paddle. That's where you come in."

"I do?"

"You're our paddle."

I'm trying to breathe here, I really am. I think she just offered me a job. I'd respond but I'm too busy freaking out.

"There will be a probationary period until you can join the tenure track. But I have faith in you! And since we've got the biggest freshman class coming in and no one to teach them how to write, you're all we've got. We can give you a temporary full-time position. Classes start on Tuesday."

"Tuesday? Like, tomorrow?"

"Shit creek," she says.

I nod. I understand that. But there's something niggling at me. Two things.

"Look," I say. "I so appreciate it, but I just want to be clear and upfront with you." I'm not talking in exclamation points. I love my mom, but I am not pink. "I'm engaged, but there was this video that came out and..."

"The sex tape?" she says, and it's in a tone that I think sounds like approval. "Honey, this is an art school. Clothing is sometimes optional. The students will be thrilled that they have a professor who's actually heard of sex. We don't care. What we do care about is the quality of your teaching. If you can do that, then you're in."

And I nod. I can do that. This crazy school is going to take a chance on me. I can hardly believe it. "Okay. I'm in."

I go home and try to find someone to celebrate with me. Sadie is unavailable because her babies are teething and she's too grumpy and tired to chat. Ash is working, but I bribe her by offering to make dinner. Tom texted me to report that he and his pals went out for fondue in Quebec, so naturally I've been thinking about melted cheese ever since. He's up there eating French food without me, damn it.

And, hello, fondue is a *dip*. I can blog about it.

I buy three different cheeses and white wine at the grocery. And two baguettes. And also broccoli because that's my nod to healthy eating.

The recipe calls for only one cup of wine, so I pour myself a glass while I grate cheese. Seriously, you could get nice, toned arms from making fondue. I stand at my kitchen counter and grate my way through three blocks of cheese. It's soothing.

After the first block, it occurs to me that I can treat myself to another episode of *Mr. Fixit Quick*. I've been portioning them out with as much care as Sadie took with her pot stash in college. I don't want to run out too quickly. I mean, Tom's in Quebec, so this is the only way I can watch him flexing.

Episode seven takes me by surprise, because I recognize the exterior of the house. It's Tom's place on the lake! "A real fixer-upper," he says during the first walk-through. The interior looks like a seventies time machine. There's an avocado-colored refrigerator and brown laminate countertops.

Gah—there's a shot of the boathouse! *Our* boathouse. The block of gruyère I'm grating hits the counter with a thud as the memories come floating back. I should probably be more embarrassed about the way I hurled myself at Tom that night. But watching the camera pan the boathouse, I feel happy, not sad. That night I lived out loud. No apologies. No asking permission.

It felt damn good. And that was true even before the orgasms.

The camera pulls back, and I see Tom with his hands on his hips. "This is gonna be awesome," he says. And since I've seen the finished product, I already know he's right.

I go back to grating cheese as the show unfolds. Unlike the other episodes I've watched, there's no homeowner on camera. They don't mention one, either. Tom tackles a tricky roofing problem, and I watch his biceps tense as he uses his hammer.

Because I have very little willpower, I watch the next episode too. Chandra is in this one, which dims my enjoyment. "What color palette does the owner want in the kitchen?" she asks Tom.

He gives her a sexy grin, and I'm instantly jealous. "We have a lot of latitude here," he says. "What color would *you* want to wake up to every morning, pretty lady?"

Uh-oh. I have a bad feeling about where this is going. So I top up my white wine and keep watching. And it only gets worse. Chandra can't decide on lighting fixtures for the patio, and Tom says, "Choose them as if they were for your own house."

And then they do the bedroom. "I've always wanted a sleigh bed," she says.

I watch each scene with wide eyes that are glassy with horror.

At some point Ash shows up. I pause the show and turn to her, my cheeks hot, my wineglass empty. "I... I think he renovated the Reeds Lake house for Chandra," I sputter.

Ash gives me an appraising look. "I have two questions."

"Shoot."

"Do you have any more of that wine?"

I point at the fridge.

"And have you actually met this Chandra?"

I shake my head.

"Then why does she matter if she's gone now?"

"That's three questions," I point out.

"So? What do you care if he once feathered Chandra's nest?"

"Because..." It's hard to say this aloud to my ninety-nine pound successful friend. "She's skinny and blond and super successful." *Just like you.*

"Still not seeing the problem," Ash says as she opens the wine. "Ooh, a cork! Fancy."

"I splurged. No box wine for your newly employed friend."

Ash grabs me into a hug. "Congrats! And don't be intimidated by some bitch named Chandra. She's not in the picture anymore, otherwise he wouldn't be fake-engaged to you. Can we dip stuff into melted cheese now?"

We do, and it's pretty great.

But I just can't let it go. So after dinner we watch more of *Mr. Fixit Quick*. The season finale was shot live for some reason. They make a big deal about the live shoot, and I'm uncomfortable. My skin prickles with the knowledge that something big is coming. And I'm not wrong. Just as Tom and Chandra lay the final tile in the kitchen of my dreams, he drops down onto one knee. To *propose to her.*

"Will you make me the happiest man in a tool belt?" he asks. He pulls an engagement ring out of his shirt pocket.

My heart is in my throat. I try to see if it's the same ring I'm wearing, but I can't. I can't see it because by that point I can't see anything at all. Maybe it's all the wine that Ash is pouring. She's like the Niagara Falls of the wine. Or maybe it's because my eyes are full of tears.

Even though I know intellectually that this was recorded months ago, I am horribly, irrationally jealous. This doesn't make much sense, of course, because I know Tom and this chick aren't currently engaged. But even though it happened on television, that proposal was very real. You just can't fake the hope and excitement on Tom's face. Nobody is that good of an actor.

Chandra may have fake boobs, but she got the real goods from Tom. I want to slap her with my frosting spatula and then force feed her something caloric. Like chocolate-covered bacon. Eat that, bitch!

I can't stop watching. I want to, but I can't look away.

On the screen, Chandra is grinning at Tom. She's all teeth. Really white, perfect teeth. "Get up, silly!" she squawks. "Don't be such a big kidder."

Oh. Oh no. Oh poor Tom.

My emotional roller coaster banks into a turn as Tom's face falls faster than my aunt Betty's soufflé. "Not kidding here, hon. I bought this house for you. For us."

She taps her high-heeled shoe on the tile and bites her lip. "Please stand up, Tom. This isn't funny. We'll talk about it later."

Oh, honey. My heart breaks into tiny slivers, like a piece of peanut brittle right out of the freezer.

"Damn!" Ash squeals. "That ice-cold bitch!"

"I know!"

There's a horrible, awkward pause, and Tom slowly rises to his feet. The producer must have cut to a commercial break a moment later. And season nine just...ends. We're sitting on my couch watching the credits roll.

"Note to self," Ash says, swigging her wine. "Never ask a woman to marry you on live TV."

"She didn't have to embarrass him!" I squeal.

Ash gives me a cautious glance. "I suppose she could have improvised better. But, honey, he *cornered* her. They weren't on the same page at all. How could he not know that?"

"She must not have been honest with him earlier on," I say, basing this opinion on zero facts. Seriously, if we were having this discussion about anyone else in TV-land, I would probably be agreeing with Ash right now. But instead I feel nothing but protective of Tom. Who could date him and not fall for him? Chandra must be one of those people who hates puppies. No—she's a cyborg! That would explain a lot.

"You know..." Ash looks thoughtful. "He should have told you this story before. It's not just about the sex tape for him. You're helping to paper over this train wreck, and you didn't even know it."

"It's fine," I insist. "Tom's a great guy. I'm happy to love him. For *pretend*," I add quickly.

Ash's eyebrows do that crazy thing where they angle toward you in a sinister way. "Pretend, huh?"

"Totally," I lie.

That night, I rub my fondue-filled belly as I toss and turn in bed. I have more than mixed emotions. I have churning emotions. A vortex of emotions, swimming with a school of hungry piranha. Whatever. You know what I mean.

I have to teach my first classes tomorrow afternoon, and my metaphors are clearly out of control, and I can't seem to care. I'm focused exclusively on Tom.

I'm mad at Tom for not telling me about Chandra, but I also empathize with him. How awful to redo a house for the love of your life (ouch) and then have her not love you back? *Publicly*. Ugh, the humiliation. On TV. Live. She was about as warm as a metal pole outside in February.

It killed me to see the hope on his face.

That's the part that makes me feel so ill—all that love emanating from him. He was like a little boy looking up at her expectantly, like she could make his wishes come true. She could be his safe place, when it was so clear that's what he needed.

When he proposed to me, he didn't get down on his knee. He looked at me and smiled. It *felt* so real. It felt more real than his real proposal on TV, where he asked Chandra to be part of his tool belt. I mean, what was that? *That* felt scripted. And odd. And now I'm confused all over again.

Piranha emotions. That's a thing. That's me right now. I'm

confused and I have a belly full of wine and melted cheese and I want to get rid of all of these jumbled thoughts. I have a job, though, so that's something. That's something I should focus on.

I will focus on that. Tomorrow. Probably.

Which is why it makes no sense that I reach my hand out to grab my phone and send a quick text to Tom.

ME: Sooo...I got that job. Great, right?

ME: And good luck with the shoot tomorrow.

(Pause)

ME: I made fondue but I'm sure Canada does it better.

ME: Canada does everything better.

(Longer pause, and then I think, *fuck it* and type the next text.)

ME: I miss you.

ME: For real.

Then I turn off my phone and fall into a deep, deep sleep.

37 ONCE MORE WITH FEELING

Tom

"Once more," the director says. "Really sell it to me. And...action!" The little whippersnapper snaps the clapper again.

I hate this guy for making me say the same shit four times already. But the only way out is through, so I do it anyway. "It won't be easy," I say, looking right at camera four. "How special do you think we can make this place in forty-eight hours? Special enough for six couples who are *Betrothed?*"

"And...cut! Let's have one more take, where you angle those abs toward the viewer."

I always wondered what it would feel like to really lose my mind, and now I know. It feels exactly like this.

There's a certain kind of energy on a film set—people scurrying around with lights and equipment. The chaos of combining filming with actual construction. I should be loving every minute of this. I *used* to love every minute of this, and then something changed, and I can't quite figure out when that happened.

In the early episodes it was just me, talking to the camera and then shooting whatever we worked on. But now the setup is fancier. I don't even have any input on what we're going to renovate. Mr. Fixit Quick has become Mr. Quick Stand On This Mark And Hold That Layout Square Like It's Useful.

It *is* useful, but they never show me using it.

Today my job is pretty much to look at the camera, flex my pecs, and smile. It's a plastic smile, and I have a perpetual two days' worth of beard, because that's what the audience voted worked best for me. We're shooting the introduction footage while everyone else preps the site.

I'm not allowed to get in there and get dirty anymore. And I liked getting dirty.

Now it's Shiny Shoes and his punk of a director who orchestrates everything. The director is new at this. He looks like he's about twenty years old, and the only tool he's ever held is his own.

Director Kid isn't even pretending to ask for my input in the various rooms of the lodge. I used to be the expert, but now he tells me to "just stand over there and look masculine." So that's what I've become. Mr. Fixit Quick is a mannequin.

I can't even text Brynn because I left my phone at the hotel in my rush to get here. When I arrived this morning, I went in to makeup, and since then I've done this talking-head routine for eight hours. While everyone else works around me.

It's the pits.

The only thing keeping me in check is the knowledge that we're almost done with the promo spots, and then the real work will begin. Finally. The special will be shot in a continuous roll for forty-eight hours straight. No breaks in the action. Then they'll edit it down to a two-hour special.

My stomach growls. What I really want right now is one of Brynn's Breakfast At Any Time specials. Her baked bacon dusted with brown sugar. Fresh crepes. Her sitting on my counter, her legs wrapped around me while she feeds me.

That hasn't actually happened, but what else have I got to think about while I stand here? It could happen. When I get home, I'll ask her. If she's still around. Things seem to be looking up for both her and me, so she'll probably want to drop this whole fake-engagement thing. Right when it was getting good too. She'll hand me back my heirloom ring and I'll...

My throat feels all tight. Must be time for a break.

I really need to shake off my shitty mood. I wanted to do this job.

It's my show, my baby. I made this. And here it is. I glance around the set, trying to remember how I got here.

Refurbishing homes was something I took up because I wanted to make a difference. Maybe that sounds ridiculous. I'm not good with words or feelings, but I am good with my hands.

And a home is important. I should know. I never really had one. It's supposed to be the place you can come to and feel safe and loved. It's a place where things work because you tend to them, and when you walk in the door, you can just slough off your worries from your shoulders the same way you take off a heavy winter coat.

This place, this chateau or whatever, isn't going to be anyone's home. This is nothing more than a four-page spread in a magazine, an eight-week show on network TV and, somehow, the symbol that I've completely sold out.

But now I'm stuck. I signed the contract. I'm already here. So I'll deal. And right now that means, apparently, moving my shoulder a little more to the left so that the light hits my biceps at a better angle.

"Okay, man," Director Kid says. "We've got the intro."

Thank fuck.

"Let's move on to the real deal!" The production staff gathers around, along with my crew. "We've got cameras in place?" Shiny Shoes asks. He gives Director Kid a pointed look.

"Oh! Let's have a status check. Camera one?"

"Camera one is ready," a techie confirms.

"Camera two is a go!" someone else calls. And so we know that Director Kid is capable of counting to twelve, as a dozen cameras in various locations are accounted for.

Then the director picks up his clapper. Seriously, he looks gleeful. Like the clapper is a symbol of power, and he wields it fervently. "Once the cameras start rolling, they don't go off until the wrap. We work with whatever you guys get, okay?" Heads nod everywhere.

Forty-eight hours. Just forty-eight hours to go. I've got this.

I almost had this. Almost.

At first, things are humming along. My crew and I unload three trucks full of building supplies. The show's editor will undoubtedly use that footage as a montage in fast forward. We'll look like busy ants on a hill. Busy ants who are very well paid.

After that the demolition starts. I get out my crowbar, which is always a good moment. "Let's go, boys!" I call, and both Burt and Larry grin. We do love to rip shit apart. Pulling down a few poorly placed walls is the most fun I'd had since leaving Michigan. It's therapeutic.

Demo takes us a couple of hours. At midnight I sneak away for a few hours of shut-eye, while a fresh crew comes in to sand the floors and put up some new wall board. When I wake up, it's time to put in the kitchen cabinetry and supervise the boat-sized hot tub installation. I stop worrying about the tacky nature of the reality show and just go with it. We put drink holders on a pedestal in the center of the tub, and window boxes along the edges of the new deck.

Even better—I bring in a stone mason to save the cool old chimneys which are deteriorating. Shiny Shoes and his man-child director probably don't care about restoration, but I'm not asking their opinion.

"Killer view," I say, setting my nail gun on the deck and gazing out at the mountaintops. I experience a moment of peace. This deck could be a happy place for someone. After *Betrothed* is finished ruining sixteen lives, someone else will take over this space, right? Someone who will appreciate what we'd done here.

"Hey, Tom?" Burt calls me from the doorway. "I hate to be the bearer of bad news."

"Uh-oh," I say, smiling into camera four. "Whatever it is, we'll handle it." I'm picturing a few rotted ceiling joists or some corroded pipes in the kitchen. "What kind of emergency is this? Plumbing? Electrical?"

Burt looks a little green, so I have a fleeting thought that the septic tank may be involved. "It's, uh, a personnel issue."

"Really?" I push past him into the lodge. "What kind of— Oh."

Oh.

There stands Chandra in the kitchen, her trusty book of paint swatches in her hand. She's holding a strip with four different shades of lavender up to the wall, and flipping her hair toward camera six.

I blink slowly and then refocus my eyes just to be sure I'm not hallucinating.

Fuck. She's still there. Furthermore, there are *three* cameras focusing on me right now. Several things become apparent to me in rapid succession. In the first place, I'm sweaty and covered in sawdust, while the woman who stomped on my heart with her pointy stiletto looks like she just stepped off a fashion runway. This isn't how I wanted to come face to face with my ex. I don't want to face her at all.

Secondly, there's no chance this little reunion is a coincidence, or that the network's failure to tell me they'd brought in Chandra is an oversight. No. Fucking. Way. It's a hundred percent intentional, and I'm seeing redder than ever before. As red as Pratt & Lambert's Velvet Red.

"Cut!" I holler. This shall not stand.

But it's like I didn't yell at all. The cameras don't wink off. Instead, Chandra turns in my direction, her smile plastic. "Well, hello there, Tom. Long time no see." She takes a couple of long strides toward me, her heels clicking importantly on the floorboards.

Who wears high heels on a construction site? Chandra, that's who. Reaching me, she leans in for one of her let's-pretend-I'm-French, double-cheeked kisses.

I sidestep her. Even as I'm doing it, I know I shouldn't. I'm creating more drama instead of less. But I can't help myself. Backing away, I wave my arms in the direction of the boyish director. "Cut," I say again. "This is bullshit."

Shiny Shoes and the director rush over. "You can't cut," they both say at once. "This is a continuous roll."

"It's in your contract," the smarmy producer insists, and that's when I know I've been had.

"Embarrassing me was not in my contract."

He grins, and I'm *this* close to punching him. "You work in reality TV, Tom. You always have."

Then I quit! The words are rising in my chest.

But before I can say them, the producer holds up a hand. "Your penalty for walking off the set is also in your contract. And it's a steep one."

"I fucking hate you," I say, my voice low. It's childish, and I'm not even sure who I'm talking to. The producer, partly. Chandra, for embarrassing me and then agreeing to show up here and *do it all over again.*

And myself, a little bit. For walking my stupid ass into this nightmare just because I wanted the network to tell me I was important enough to save.

When will I ever learn?

Shiny Shoes doesn't even look offended. He must be really good at his job, because drama rolls off this chump like rain from a standing-seam roof. "Doesn't matter how you feel about me," he says with a shrug. "But I'll make a deal with you. Get back to work. I'll edit out your little tantrum if you man up and finish this project with Chandra. Just turn around and walk out that door—" He points toward the deck. "—and walk back in here and greet her. Do it *now.*"

The way he adds that last bit is just meant to demean me. Like I'm his teenage son who needs to ask daddy for the car keys.

There is a deep silence on the set. Every camera operator, every crew member is watching. Even the day laborers we've hired to haul away the extra scraps of wallboard. They're all waiting to see if I'll unman myself by tucking my tail between my legs and doing what the producer wants. Or whether I'll go all diva and make a big stink or throw construction materials around like an angry monkey.

That second thing sounds pretty appealing.

I glance up at Chandra. She's standing there with her skinny arms folded across her chest, pushing her inflated boobs up to her chin and looking smug. This woman never loved me. How could she? She's made of glass. I can see that now. She just wanted to hitch her wagon to a successful TV show and get everything she could from me. Now she's back for more.

Everyone wants something from me. And right now they want me to make a scene. If I kick over the grouting tray in frustration or start yelling, they'll use that in their promo spots. *Watch Tom Spanner lose it after this message from our sponsor!*

I take a deep breath and find my resolve. I won't give them the satisfaction. I won't feed the beast.

Standing up as straight as I possibly can, I turn around and walk out the door. On the deck outside, I count to ten, taking more deep breaths. Dawn is creeping towards us. There's a warm light tinting the horizon.

I'm trying to see something. An image. I'm not quite sure what yet, so I wait a few moments until it becomes clear. I picture Brynn asleep in her bed in that little Victorian house she rents, her foot kicked out from the covers to balance out her body heat, and that's the image I carry back inside with me. That bare foot. The curve of her sleeping form.

I step into the kitchen again. "Well, hello," I say to Chandra. "Fancy meeting you here."

She blinks. Then she blinks again. Or maybe it's her fake eyelashes. They are so enormous that it looks like she's blinking twice. Clearly, though, I've taken her by surprise. She obviously assumed I wouldn't do exactly what the producer said. "Hi," she finally manages. "...Tom." She adds my name too late, and it makes her sound like an imbecile. "How've you been?"

"Terrific!" I boom, because it's finally true. The first months after Chandra dumped me were awful. But since I stopped brooding, I've been pretty happy. Brynn made life more fun.

"That's good." She swallows hard, and I see her straighten her spine and try to pull herself together. "Nice lodge, right? I've been thinking about a lavender color scheme."

Here's where, according to the script that we've followed in every episode, I agree with her. She's the decorating genius, the one with all the brains, and I'm just the brawn.

"I think that sounds perfectly awful!" I say, giving camera number three a big smile. "If I were the designer, I'd pick a medium ochre. Something that's actually warm and inviting. But if you want to make the place look like a bedroom from the Pottery Barn Teen catalogue, you go right ahead and amuse yourself."

Across the room, Burt doubles over with laughter. I must be doing something right.

Two steps forward brings me to Chandra. I lean in and kiss her on her emaciated cheek. "Good chat, honey!" I walk off, toward Burt. And I can feel the cameras zooming in on Chandra's stunned face.

God, I'm over her. And I'm over the rest of this too. But in less than forty-eight hours it won't matter. I'll be on my way home.

38 FIERCE

Brynn

My phone rings, and I actually dance across the room to pick it up.

But the caller isn't Tom.

My heart deflates like a whoopee cushion—suddenly and with great force, but without the noise. Thankfully. It's been half a day since I texted Tom. I told Tom I missed him, and he didn't respond.

I'm trying not to be crushed, because New Brynn is the kind of girl who's getting her shit together.

"I'm a strong woman, living my life the way I want!" I chant to the ceiling fan.

The ceiling fan has no reply.

Meanwhile, the caller tries again. *Bracken and Smith*, the caller ID says. That sounds a little familiar so I answer it.

"Hello?"

"Good day." The voice on the other end is clipped, and I'm instantly wary. "We represent Mr. Steven Masters in the matter of his divorce."

Oh, lovely. Steven's divorce lawyer. Just what a girl needs. "How can I help you?" I ask slowly. Like, really slowly. *Howwww cannn I helllllp yooooooooou?* Divorce lawyers charge in six-minute increments. I always made a point of taking up as much of Steven's lawyers' time as I could.

A girl has to have her fun where she can find it.

"Mr. Masters is filing a motion to renegotiate his alimony payment."

"Reallllllyyyy?" The lawyer probably thinks I have a speech impediment. "Why would he dooooooo that?" Steven barely pays me anything, since we're both employable adults with no kids. But he kept our house, so he owes me for that.

"Your remarriage," he says icily. "It will change the terms of your divorce."

"That's ridiculous," I say, forgetting to speak slowly. "I'm not remarried."

"According to the news media—"

"Really? Your investigator quit, huh? My marital status is single until further notice. And Steven owes me for half the house, no matter what."

"It doesn't even matter," the dickwad on the other end of this call says. "If you were sexually intimate with your new fiancé prior to the official separation, he can still sue you."

"But I wasn't!"

"We can analyze the phone records from the time before your divorce—"

"Do it!" I shriek. "Please. Take all the time you need. I'll fax you our Verizon bills, going back a couple of years. Would five years be enough? Also, you may want to talk to your *client* and see who he was involved with before we ended our relationship." I'm shaking, but not because I'm scared. I did nothing wrong. Not one thing. And if my ex thinks so little of me, then I hope he spends a thousand billable hours trying to shame me. I don't actually know for sure that he was involved with someone, but if he wants to play hardball, I will.

"A lawsuit could be very costly," the voice reminds me. "It might be easier for everyone if I just send over a document of agreement, changing the terms of your alimony."

"Fuck. Right. Off," I say immediately. "Steven will pay every penny he owes. On time. And then I *might* not sue his family for wrongful termination at the college. If I'm feeling generous." There's a pause. Even though he's quiet, I can tell he's struggling with what to say. Because I'm absolutely right.

Ash has already urged me to sue—to hold Steven's asshole father accountable for my pink slip. I'm pretty sure I was the only one in my department to get one. I hate the idea of suing anybody. But suddenly I hate it a little less.

There's a click on the line.

"Hello?" I ask.

The lawyer actually hung up on me.

I sit there a minute, stunned. Then I reach for the landline I never use and dial Steven's cell phone from memory. He probably doesn't know this number, and he might just answer.

It works.

"Hello?" he asks in his stupid, quavery voice.

"This is Brynn," I say, trying to keep the growl out of my voice. "I never cheated. Not once. Even though you ignored me for years."

"Oh. Uh..." I've caught him off guard. Clearly he didn't expect to have to deal with me, even over the phone. "Well..."

"Your father fired me. He took my job. I have *no income except for the money you rightfully owe me from our house*. If you come after that, I will sue your father. Very publicly. Very painfully. And if the *West Michigan Press* asks me for a statement, I will be sure to add that your penis resembles an alien noodle. And that you don't have the first clue how to use it."

He gasps. "There's no need to be cruel."

"Oh really? Well it's *cruel* to treat your wife like the house elf, Steven! If my rage bubbles over, just remember that it comes from someplace very real. I was a competent, optimistic human being until you wore me down."

He is silent for a moment. "You didn't cheat? That video was pretty, er... Revealing."

My heart gallops as I picture Steven watching the video. Then hitting *play* again and again. I *almost* giggle, but rein it in at the last second. It sounds like a burp, but whatever. "You watched the video?"

"Well, er... My father..."

Another half giggle escapes into my throat, and I swallow it down. "Your father enjoyed it too, huh?"

"Um..." Steven makes an embarrassed noise. "The tabloids say you met Tom Spanner in the spring."

"*That's* your issue? Daddy read the tabloids, and now you think I'm a cheater? The tabloids also say that Chris Hemsworth is from the planet Uranus!" I'd read it last week in the grocery store checkout.

Uranus is a funny word.

Also, holy crap, let this day go down in history. For the first time in way too long, I actually spat out a witty rejoinder instead of stewing over it six hours later, lying sleepless and angry in my bed. This is a turning point! I need wine to celebrate.

Furthermore, I'm going to have to frame that issue of *The Sun* featuring Chris Hemsworth and his spacecraft. For posterity.

"Look, I'm not supposed to be talking to you," Steven says abruptly, as if he's just realized he's been beaten. "We can communicate through our lawyers."

"Great idea! Have yours call me directly." I am on fire, bitches. "I had so much fun chatting with him earlier. I hope he charges you a hundred grand to prove that I never cheated on your wimpy, pale white ass."

Then? I hang up. On Steven. For the first time in my life, I'm not waiting for his approval. Old Brynn would actually be worried right now about his prying and his stupid lawyer's phone call. But New Brynn does not have time for that kind of bullshit.

I pump my fist in the air for the first time since... Well, ever.

Then I actually find "Eye of the Tiger" on YouTube, play it, and pump my fist again.

It's just that kind of a moment.

39 A BLUR, A BIKINI, AND A MOMENT OF TRUTH

Tom

The continuous shoot becomes a blur. I'm exhausted, running on coffee and instinct. This must be how marathon runners feel.

Like a good boy, I stand where they tell me to. We demolish the living room and then a whole team comes in to start rebuilding. But it's not really rebuilding. This is a spit and polish job. We get the fucking hot tub fully operational. I've at least convinced them to do a rustic-looking cedar wrap-around, and so I start cutting the staves.

It's very satisfying splitting wood with a power tool.

Chandra comes out wearing a tiny orange bikini, her breasts threatening to leap out of the top at any second. The camera pans to me to get my reaction. I say, "Hey, Chandra, can you hand me that two-by-four?" I don't even look at her.

She huffs and says, "But I'm ready for us to...get wet."

"Shower still works inside," I offer.

The camera pans away. Nothing to see here.

On break, there are donuts and piles of fruit, but there's nothing to dip it in. If there was a dip here, everything would be better.

Naturally, my thoughts turn to Brynn again. If she were here, I'd be neck deep in that hot tub in a hot second. She'd probably wear some kind of one-piece suit with strings that I could slowly undo. There's something appealing about that. How she's covered up but all

I need to do is reach over and, with a few careful motions of my fingers, she can unfurl before me.

And I'm glad the camera isn't on me now because my face is hot and my dick is hard.

About time, my dick says. *I thought you forgot about me.*

I tell him to relax. I have plenty of time for him, but it needs to be around the right person.

And that person is in Michigan right now.

Twenty-four hours to go.

The producers are frustrated because there's not enough drama. Not enough conflict. Director Kid says, "Look, we're half through this and all we've got is you working on the house. This is a snoozefest. You've got to give us *something.*"

"My contract didn't mention anything about giving you 'something.' It just mentioned refurbishing this house. And that's what I'm doing."

I take a nap on the cot while the crew lays down cool marble for the floors. They're taking out all the warm earth tones, the stuff that made this place feel rustic and inviting, and they're making everything gray with accents of lilac. Every change they make sucks out the life of this place a little more.

The nap doesn't help. I keep waking up.

And then there's a tap on my shoulder. A sharp tap with a manicured nail. Those things are fucking sharp. Maybe they're a survival mechanism. She could open cans with them. I open my eyes, but I didn't need to. I can smell Chandra's perfume even before she enters the room.

"Hey," she says.

I sit up, and she lowers herself down next to me.

"I didn't want to come here, you know."

"Okay," I say warily.

"But..." She shrugs. "I can't seem to get my own show, and this offer was..."

"Too good to pass up," I finish for her.

"Yeah."

We're quiet. It's not as awkward as it should be. I can sense she needs to tell me something, so I just wait it out.

"I'm sorry," she says. It's a surprise to hear her say it. I'm not sure what she's sorry for exactly, so I wait some more. "Maybe I should've said yes on camera, when you asked me to marry you. The producers wanted me to say yes. I was going to do it. We worked so well together on set. We look great together. We'd have attractive kids. But..."

"But what?" I ask it softly. Well, as softly as I can. I'm not mad anymore. I'm not anything really, except maybe mildly curious.

"But then we went live, and something stopped me. You were perfectly nice and we had fun together, but I just always felt like something was missing, between us. And when you asked me to marry you, I just sort of blanked out. They want us back together, you know. That's why I'm here. I'll get a big bonus if I can seduce you."

Wait, what?

That's when I start to sputter. "You can't! No way! I'm..." I almost say "in love with someone" and that surprises me a little. But she doesn't let me finish.

"It's okay. The thing is, as much as I'd like the bonus, I'd rather have something that's...real."

I look at her then, and I smile. She reaches for my hand, and I take it. We're just sitting there next to each other. It's sort of awkward, but it's maybe the first genuine moment we've ever shared. I give her hand a squeeze, and then I let go. We let go.

Then she says something that really does surprise me. "And to tell you the truth, I fucking hate lilac."

I'll be on my way back to Michigan by the time I find out that they were filming us.

40 TOP TEN. AGAIN. BECAUSE LISTS ARE SATISFYING.

Brynn: Top Ten Best Things in Life This Week

1. The new Chris Hemsworth photo on my wall. I colored the spaceship purple before I took it to the framing shop.

2. Walking through a giant vagina to buy coffee. It's like re-experiencing my own birth every time I need caffeine.

3. Dips and balls. Because even though I am now properly employed, those never go out of style.

4. Food on sticks. Because I'm expanding my horizons.

5. Feeling competent.

6. Actually *being* competent. (Since #5 seems to apply to men, regardless.)

7. The afterglow of telling Steven to fuck off. I'm still glowing. I don't even need to turn on lamps after dark.

8—10. Being too busy having a life to finish this list.

41 PUZZLE PIECES & RAMEN NOODLES

Brynn

There's a certain satisfaction that happens when you're doing something you're good at. It's that satisfying "snick" of a puzzle piece sliding into place. When I walk through the giant, comforting vagina and into my classroom on Tuesdays and Thursdays, I feel that snick. I'm where I need to be. And I am good at this.

There's twenty hungry students. I mean that literally. I think they're all existing on art, sex, and ramen noodles, and I want to make them all some homemade ravioli. I'll save that for later in the semester. First, though, I want to get them thinking about words. How they work. What they can do. How they can change your life.

This week I'm not flighty or unfocused or boring, or any of the things I felt like I was when I was with Steven.

When I go over the syllabus, and I give out the first assignment, I'm confident. Controlled. Trembling a little with excitement. Great things will happen in this place, because I'm where I need to be.

By Thursday night, I've finished teaching for the week, so I can relax. And by relax, I mean I text Sadie and Ash to come over so we can watch *Mr. Fixit Quick Does Quebec*. I'm cooking up some snacks, and

Sadie has convinced her husband to watch the babies for the night so she can have a moment to recharge. I haven't heard from Ash yet, but she's always up for a party.

While making a béchamel sauce for the new dip I'm creating, I think about Tom. I am a little sad that I haven't heard from him for two days, but he warned me that continuous shooting wouldn't leave him time to check his phone. And he wasn't sure about cell reception in the woods.

But I miss him, damn it. The moonstone on the ring glimmers. I'm going to be really sad to give it up. And I'm still curious about its origins. I'm wearing an old story on my finger. I just know it.

There's a knock at the door and then a string of curses. So I know Ash has arrived.

"What's wrong this time?" I ask as I let her in.

"There's no more media hounding your doorstep? Those fuckers. How are we going to keep your cookbook sales up if you're not newsworthy?"

I'm definitely excited that the vultures are gone, but I keep that to myself. "The cookbook sales were always going to be a temporary phenomenon. I'm just happy to have the one-time boost, you know? If you still want to go to Florida at New Years, I can totally say yes now."

"We're going, bitch." She waves around the pink leather planner that she carries everywhere. "I inked it in and used one of my favorite travel stickers."

"Oh. Well. I wouldn't want to fuck with your planner pages."

"You really wouldn't," she says, missing my irony. She gives me the once-over. "Put a dress on. You can't go out drinking in that."

I look down at my comfy jeans. "I don't need a dress to watch the show with you guys. I made food on sticks. That's a party right there."

She stalks past me into the kitchen and grabs a skewer of yakitori chicken off a platter. She nibbles on it. "These are awesome. Now go put on a dress. There's a cool party we're going to crash."

I feel an immediate flutter in my nether regions, because that's how I met Tom. The classic love story, right? Crashing a party led to boathouse sex led to the world seeing my sex tape. Which led to a fake engagement. Every girl's dream.

Wait...

"I'm not going," I say.

"Yeah you are." Ash grabs another skewer.

"Nope. Have to watch my show."

She gives me a pitying look. "I know you're hung up on him, sweetie. But that's why you must. Get back on that horse."

"No can do."

She eats the rest of the yakitori, washes her hands and marches upstairs. I know she'll come downstairs with a wrap dress and some of my new, sexy underwear. The lingerie I bought for Tom. I was tempted to get the underwear with little foxes all over them, but the lace thong was sexier. Then I thought, *fuck it*, and bought the foxes too. Balance.

For the hundredth time I check my phone, but there's no text from him. He's probably busy wrapping up his Quebec special. Or maybe he's composing his Dear Brynn letter. Tom's a good guy. When he decides we're officially done, he'll be super nice about it.

I'll be sad even so.

Ash returns with a pink wrap dress, and I fuss about the color and then put it on anyway.

Fucking girlfriends.

42 UP ON THE ROOFTOP

Brynn

"If they don't have a TV here, I'm leaving," I threaten as we step into the elevator.

"If they don't have a TV, you can watch your show on my iPad," Ash says. "Of course, that will make you the sad girl who's sitting in the corner of a decadent private rooftop party watching a home renovation show on her iPad."

"And *you'll* be the superbitch who points that out," I snap.

"Stop squabbling," Sadie says, whipping a lipstick out of her clutch purse. "This is my big night out, so get along or I'll tell you gross stories about diaper blowouts."

That's a pretty good threat, so Ash and I hug. Then she and Sadie check their lipstick in the reflective surface of the elevator panel. It's the shiniest elevator I've ever seen. They should pass out sunglasses because the glare is killer.

"Where are we, exactly?" I ask as the car rises forever upward.

"The VanHeimlich building," she answers. Telling me nothing.

Ash has given me very few details of this party, either because A) she doesn't know anything about it, or B) she has something to hide. It's probably that second thing. I can only pray we're not crashing a wedding. Or a funeral. That would actually be worse. And who throws a party on the top of a downtown office building?

"Why?" I try, because I should really ask more questions.

"There's a new bar opening on top of the building. And they just put in some hotel suites for visiting dignitaries. None of it is open yet. This is their private preview night."

"Oh!" That actually sounds fun. "Are we invited, or should I prepare a story about how I know the VanHeimlich family?" They're a family of billionaires who own half of Grand Rapids.

"We're invited. There's a secret password. Just watch."

The doors finally part. I expect to see a lobby or a hallway, so I'm stunned to step out onto...a lawn. There's grass growing on top of this tall building. It's heaven! I see a grand water fountain, in which several partygoers are actually wading. And a bocce court! And a beanbag toss! There's a long maple bar under a sleek awning. And since we're on top of a building, there are views for miles.

Leaving the house is awesome. Who knew?

We are stopped immediately by Braht. No—not Braht. It's his younger twenty-something clone. Same blond hair and blueblood features. Same linen jacket over shorts with lobsters embroidered into the fabric. Same boat shoes and attitude. But this edition is giving Ash a frowny face instead of panting like a dog in heat. "Password, please," Braht's Mini-Me says.

"Wankapin," Ash replies cooly.

"Wait. *Wankapin?*" I chortle. Really—I totally chortled. It happens.

But Little Braht gives me an icy stare. "It's a flowering plant native to the Central American wetlands."

"Wetlands!" I giggle.

He glares.

The real Braht comes bounding over, pushes his clone aside, and sweeps his hand toward the bar. "Come in! Come in! Don't let Bramly slow you down."

"Bramly?"

He growls.

"Is there champagne?" Ash demands, her spine as straight as the VanHeimlich building. Braht has the weirdest effect on my friend. I just don't understand it. He turns her Bitch Meter right up to eleven.

"Of course, milady. Step right this way."

She sort of sneers at him, and I trail along, admiring the rooftop lawn. The grass pokes my toes through my sandals. I wonder how they mow up here. And can weeds even travel up to the thirtieth floor?

The bartenders are all wearing white shirts to show off their tans. They're so clean-cut that it's distracting. Their teeth shine so brightly I almost need shades.

"Champagne?" a bartender asks, flashing me his gleaming smile.

I plunk down on a bar stool. "Of course!" I say all hoity-toity like. "I always drink champagne on rooftop lawns, darling!"

The irony goes right over the poor thing's carefully styled hair. "Coming right up!"

When my champagne arrives, it tastes phenomenal. Even better —I spot a TV screen over the bar. Though it's currently dark. "Pardon me, young sir." I wave down the nearest Ken doll. "Would it be possible for you to tune that television to H&G? My fiancé's special is on tonight." That's right—I'm namedropping to see Tom on the tube. But these are desperate times. "Have you seen *Mr. Fixit Quick?*"

Ken Doll has no idea what I'm talking about. But he hands me a remote control with another blinding smile and then moves off to make a Tom Collins for someone.

"These bacon-wrapped scallops are divine," Ash says. She sets a tiny plate in front of me. "Drink up, honey. I got you another glass of bubbly."

Life is really good here on the rooftop. Tom's show flickers to life above me. There's no sound, but that's okay. I don't need sound to admire Tom in his tight-fitting T-shirt, directing the delivery of a truckload of two-by-fours. He hammers a cross-piece to a stud, and when his biceps flex, I feel it in my nipples.

Also, bacon-wrapped scallops *are* divine. I pull my notebook out of my bag and add "Wrapped and Stuffed Things" to my Top Ten List in progress.

There is a montage of Tom and his guys demolishing stuff. Walls come down. Windows are added. There's a big deck outside with killer views. It's romantic. When I see him standing alone at the railing, looking out at the mountains, he looks lonely.

During the commercial break, I let Ash introduce me to some of Braht's friends. They have names like Buck and Chandler. One of them is a VanHeimlich, and I study him to see if I can tell he's a billionaire.

Nope. Just another preppy with an expensive watch. They all look alike to me.

I drink more champagne. Sneaking my phone out of my bag, I check the screen. It's blank. Tom still hasn't called or texted.

But, hey. I knew this would eventually happen. He just got his career back, and so did I. This was the plan all along, right? The newer, more confident Brynn can handle this disappointment, even if Tom was really very special.

I'm done pining for men who don't want me. New Brynn doesn't do that.

New Brynn does, however, keep the fancy bar's remote control in her purse. Just in case they feel like cutting off my TV privileges. And as soon as Ash allows me, I retreat to my bar stool for another hit of Tom.

Everyone has celebrity crushes, right? I'm not being obsessive.

Tom installs a ridiculous hot tub on the deck. Shamu's tank is smaller than this eyesore. Tom actually rolls his eyes at it. I don't even need the sound track to hear his disdain.

One of Tom's buddies sticks his head out of the door and beckons. His face is grim, and I sit up straight, wondering what's gone wrong.

When the camera cuts to a smirking Chandra, I almost drop my champagne glass.

"Uh-oh," Sadie says from over my shoulder.

I watch while Tom greets Chandra. I can't hear what's said. But he kisses her on the cheek and then walks away.

"It's only a cheek kiss," Sadie points out. "And, analyzing his body language, that was a reluctant cheek kiss, anyway."

The show cuts to a commercial.

Feeling a little lightheaded, I turn around and survey the crowd. There's a bocce game going on, two competitors in penny loafers are tossing their balls together.

Their *bocce* balls. Because even though this is a great party, it's not that kind of party.

I think about the last party my friends dragged me to—when my ex had walked in and I'd lost my marbles. Good thing, too. Because that's how I'd met Tom.

But my life doesn't need a repeat. There's no boathouse, for starters. More to the point, there's no Tom. I scan the crowd and find that I'm surrounded by a sea of people who like to golf. None of them know how to handle a nail gun. I can just tell. Some of these men get manicures more frequently than I do.

"What are you looking for?" Sadie asks the question cautiously, the way you speak to someone who might not be okay.

"Tom," I sigh. "I'm looking for Tom. I... I think I'm in love with him."

"Uh-oh!" Ash says, swooping in. "Here. Do a shot." She waves at one of the bartenders. "We have a tequila emergency over here!"

"No we don't," I say firmly. My eyes travel back to the TV screen. I see Tom on a bed of some kind, and my heart flops over like one of my mother's Jell-O molds. Chandra sits down beside him. They're touching!

I let out a tiny shriek of dismay.

"Salt, tequila, then lime," Ash recites with the same urgency a fireman uses to say stop, drop, and roll.

But no. Hold your tequila and don't pull the pin on your fire extinguishers. Because even though I can't hear the program, I know what endings look like. I've had endings, and they look like Tom and Chandra on that screen. He's saying something nice, and she's looking wistful.

Then she gets up and walks away.

"Yeah!" All three of us throw our arms in the air and cheer. Heads turn as preppies look over to see if maybe there's a baseball game on. But it's just Tom on the screen, getting up to check some tile grout.

"He's mine," I say out loud. Then I say it again because apparently once wasn't creepy enough. "MINE." Then, "I'm doing this. I'm going after him, even though he hasn't texted me back. Even though his plane was supposed to land an hour ago, and I haven't heard a word." The thing is, Tom loves me too. I can feel it in my belly, right near the bacon-wrapped scallops.

"Oh, wow," Ash says. "This wasn't supposed to happen. He was supposed to be your rebound fuck."

"He was the antidote to your red flag! Remember, you really

shouldn't trust your instincts for a while," Sadie offers. She means well, but....

"Doesn't matter," I say, throwing back that shot of tequila she ordered me. Because tequila shouldn't go to waste even when your life isn't really ending.

Ash hands me the lime and shakes her head. "This won't end well. True love doesn't happen, honey." Her eyes dart to the side. "Except to Sadie," she amends quickly. Because it's rude to tell your married friend that her life is a farce.

"Not even to Sadie," Sadie mumbles. Then she grabs another shot off the bar and drinks it.

Ash hands a lime to Sadie, who looks like she needs that tequila at least as badly as I do.

"Well..." Ash puts her hands on her tiny hips. "I suppose it would only be fair to tell you that I put your phone into airplane mode right when I arrived at your place two hours ago. So you wouldn't be distracted by texts from your mom when you were hoping to hear from Tom."

For a second I just blink at her. Then I wrench open my purse, toss out the remote control, and grab the phone. I turn off airplane mode and say a quick prayer.

The thing floods with texts. Half are from my mother, wondering how to pronounce the word "gif." But there are several from Tom! *Where are you? I'm outside your house.*

I hit the call button. "Tom?" I gasp when he answers. "You're back!"

"I missed you, baby. Where are you?"

"On a rooftop! At this weird party. Braht is here and—"

The call drops.

"Damn it!" I scream. "We have to leave. Tom is looking for me."

"We can't," Ash says. "Your driver needs an hour before her two glasses of bubbly wear off. I didn't have any tequila or we'd be here until midnight."

Damn her and her zero percent body fat.

Okay, there's always Uber. But where to ask them to take me? Tom's house? Mine? I need a location. I need a big, romantic reunion. I'm due, damn it. Tom and I running toward each other across a meadow filled with daisies. Or Tom and I leaping over suitcases in the airport to reach each other.

Or Tom and I buck naked in a boathouse. I'm not picky, as long as he's there. And naked.

"Gotta go, ladies," I say, dropping a tip onto the bar and winking at the bartender. "I have people to see and sex to have."

I take off running. Why am I running? Because I know what I want, and I want Tom and that means I want him now! I am clearing the perfectly manicured rooftop patio, bee-lining down the endless lawn towards the brushed metal elevators.

I press the button on the elevator. Nothing lights up. *Come on, fucker.* I press it a few more times just to show it who's boss. And then I hear a whir, and a strip of blue light zips around the elevator, maybe signifying takeoff. I don't know. I need to focus. I'm so stirred up, certain that the only thing that will calm me down is a bowl of chocolate soup, or sex with Tom. Orrrrrr, sex with Tom in a bowl of chocolate soup.

Now I really can't focus.

I reach into the gap of my dress and adjust my boobs They need it. Plus, it comforts me. So when the elevator door dings and slides open, there I am, standing with my hand firmly wrapped around my breast and holy fuck if it isn't Tom, grinning right at me.

The blue lights sparkle.

43 SIR FIXIT DICK IS EXCITED

Tom

The only thing I register in my sleep-deprived and stressed-out haze is that the elevator doors have slid open with a slight snick and flashing lights, like I'm about to enter the main deck of the Enterprise. When those doors snick open, I have to admit, I'm a little startled. There is this gorgeous, curvy, delicious woman staring at me as she fondles her breast. And then I laugh, because what else can you do?

What happens next surprises me, and that's saying something. Brynn takes one look at me, releases her breast, and says in this voice that seems to come from the bottom of a well, or maybe from her inner wolf, "MIIIIIIINNNNNNNEEE." And then she pounces. It's déjà vu all over again to the boathouse.

This time, though, I'm ready for her.

She leaps, wraps her legs around me, and my big hands enfold her and go straight to her ass where I heft her up a bit, so I can have a better hold, because right now, and for a very long while, I'm going to hold on to this woman. I hear her growl one more time and then she's sucking my face. I mean that literally. She's like that alien pod thing in *Alien*, only, you know, the version of an alien that is super-hot and totally fuckable.

I suck her face right back. In the elevator. The doors slide closed and then I'm all over her and she's all over me and...

Fuck.

We're in an elevator.

"Baby," I manage.

"Shut up," she says. And she kisses my lips, my neck, my ear. Then she tugs open my dress shirt a little at the top and kisses my clavicle, so I push the button to floor number thirty, the penthouse, where Braht has already reserved my room.

It's like he knew or something.

Whatever, I'm not questioning it because—

I AM GOING TO MAKE SWEET LOVE TO MY WOMAN FOR HOURS, my dick shouts.

Sweet love? Huh.

Then I nod, and then my face is in her cleavage and my tongue and my hands are doing things, and my dick is so happy he's humming. Or vibrating. Whatever. Sir Fixit Dick is excited.

When the doors ding and slide open again, I let her feet slide to the floor and stop kissing her just long enough to look at her so I know she is real. Her hair is mussed and her breasts are heaving against her fucking wrap dress, and I don't think I've ever been happier.

For now.

But I'm pretty sure I'm going to be even happier in a few minutes.

"What?" she asks.

"Penthouse," I say. "I have. Key."

"Oh. Yes!" And then we're kissing again.

There's the plastic key card, a slide, a fumble, and we fall into the room. I shut the door. She's undressing me and I'm unwrapping her. It's Christmas every day with this woman! God, I fucking love her.

She stops abruptly.

"You do?" she asks, and either I said that out loud or she can read my mind. It doesn't matter.

"Brynn, yes. God. Somewhere between the boathouse and your fondness for appetizers, I fell for you. Hard. And...I'm in love with you. I want you. I want what we have to be real—"

She interrupts. "It is real, all of it." She rips my shirt all the way open, flinging buttons everywhere. It's very butch, and I know I've found the woman for me. She tugs my shirt off so I'm bare-chested, and she is standing there in a push-up bra and these tiny panties that leave too much to the imagination, so I yank on them until she's free. So much better. I don't have the patience for imagining anything with her.

"I love you too," she says. "Big love. For your big hands. Out of words right now, so..."

I breathe for a minute. I do, because I don't want to fuck this up. "Can I make love to you now?"

She tilts her head. "If you mean make love to me by fucking me and really meaning it, then yes. I love you too. Did I say that?"

"You did." I reach behind her and unclasp her bra. She let it drops to the floor. She pulls my pants and boxers down and I kick them off. My dick is at full, uhm, staff. Salute. Whatever. It's bigger and harder than it's ever been. So I point to it. "Get on this. Now."

44 FINALLY

Tom's Dick

Yes! What he said! Come to papa! Last one in is a...
    Ahhhhhh. Right...there.
    Finally.

45 PILLOW TALK

Brynn

Tom has the hotel room for the whole weekend. I don't understand why, and so I ask him while we're lying in bed together, me snuggled into him, my hand playing with the hair on his chest. He's such a *man,* you know? "Why did you get a hotel when you have your huge cold mansion in East Grand Rapids?"

"That answers it right there."

"It does?"

"You said huge. Cold. Mansion."

"I did?"

"Yes."

"Well, that was rude of me. Even if it's true. That place has no soul. Except the boathouse. I could live in that boathouse. Or the kitchen."

I seem to have lost my filter. That's what happens when you're sexually satisfied and curled up beside the right guy. You stop worrying about every little thing.

"That place isn't me," he says. "Well, it's not me now. It was me... when I was trying to be perfect."

"You seem pretty perfect to me."

"Perfect *for* you, maybe." He smiles. I snuggle in a little closer.

"I'm going to ask Braht to put it on the market. After I do a little more work on it."

"Really?"

"Yep. I'm done with that place. It took me nine seasons of *Mr. Fixit Quick* to realize that you can't build a home out of luxury tile and premium cabinetry. I've been trying to do that for a long time." He picks up my hand and admires the moonstone, seemingly lost in thought.

"Here's a question, though." I should be panicking now, but I'm not. "If you sell your mansion, where will you live?"

"Hmmm." He rubs his hand down my arm, and I start to tingle all over again. "I was thinking..." *Rub-rub.* "There's this delightful Victorian in Eastown with a banister that really needs some attention."

"Does it?"

"Its floor is slanted and needs some help. And the kitchen needs to be updated."

"It probably needs to be really updated. It needs to double in size. But I don't own that place, remember?" Do I? I'm feeling a little lightheaded because I think he just implied that he wanted to move in with me.

Last week that would have sounded scary, but I'm starting to realize it's not. Relationships are awesome with someone like Tom in your life.

He rubs my stomach, and I feel lazier than a cat in the sun.

"I'm going to buy another place, Brynn. And this one won't be cold. I know it's a lot to ask, but maybe I could spend some time at your place while I'm between houses?"

"I like that idea a lot," I whisper.

"Yeah?"

"Yeah..." I'm trying to focus on what he's saying and not that, while he's stroking me, the covers covering his legs are starting to tent.

"I want a cottage on Lake Michigan," he says.

"Wow, really?"

"Really. Unless you hate that idea. Because wherever I'm going, I'm hoping to take you with me."

Right now I have to say something to him. Something big and

scary. The thing is, though, I want to do things right this time, and that means being honest and vulnerable. Showing my tender belly in the hopes that he'll rub it.

"I'll go with you," I say. "But the thing is, I don't want you to make a home for me."

He shifts a little, there's this pause, and then, "You don't?" He sounds hurt. But I'm not finished.

"I want you to make a home *with* me." I let that sink in. I can feel him relax into the idea.

"You mean like partners?"

"More like a family. You and me."

He kisses me softly in response.

This is a very exciting idea. Almost as exciting as the tent Tom is pitching beside me. Cottages and tents are my new favorite things. "Ungh. I want you and all of that. And a really big kitchen. I've got big plans for my website. I've been thinking of doing some videos... since the, uhm, last one went viral."

"Are you going to cook naked?"

"Only for you. I'll wear an apron, though."

"Just an apron?"

"One with a really long tie..."

And then we stop talking because... Well, because we both decide to get lucky. And we get lucky all morning long.

It's many hours later.

Fine, it's two days later.

And an hour ago I promised myself I'd get up and go home. Not because I want to. Not because Tom wants me to. But because I have a staff meeting to go to and prep work to do before this week's classes.

"Hey, Tom." I am admiring the moonstone in the filtered hotel light. "Now will you tell me about the ring? I'm still curious." We haven't talked about our fake engagement at all. We've spent the weekend together naked, with no time for something as silly as plans.

Tom rolls over and kisses my shoulder. "Maybe."

"Maybe?"

"I'll tell you about it someday. We need time."

"It's a long story?"

"No. But I'm hoping that you and I become a long story. And if we do, I want you to know the story of the ring, and to know why it means so much to me."

I slide it off my finger and offer it to him. "Maybe you'd rather take care of it."

Tom shakes his head. He reaches up and closes my hand around the ring. "You hang on to it. Someday I hope you decide you could marry me for real. But I know better now than to rush the question. We have time."

I suck in a breath. I'm glad he isn't asking me to talk about marriage right this second. I have a really good feeling about the two of us, but the ink is barely dry on my divorce papers. "It still stings that I didn't get marriage right on the first try."

"Yeah? Well, I proposed to someone I wasn't in love with. I'd have the same regrets as you do, except she was smart enough to shut me down."

"She didn't have to be cruel, though." I'll always defend my man.

"Eh. I'm over it," he insists.

"What a couple of fuckups we are."

"Not anymore, gorgeous." He kisses my neck. "We've got it right this time."

I let him worship my neck for a little longer, until he shifts his hips suggestively. I lower my mouth to his ear and whisper hotly, "Tell me about the ring."

"You're sneaky," he chuckles. "But you'll hear about it when I'm good and ready."

I put my hand under the sheet and give him a stroke. "Did someone say ready?"

He rolls on top of me, and it's another hour until I finally leave.

At the door, he pulls me close to him and gives me one of those kisses that makes my toes curl. Literally. And then they cramp up, because in real life that's what happens. "I have to go," I say. "But I'll come back."

Just as I start to walk down the hallway he calls out "About the ring?"

Holy shit. I stop. I don't turn around. I just wait.

"It's the only thing of value in my family. Not monetary value. Sentimental. It came from my great Aunt Maddie who married a ninety-five-year-old millionaire and then ran off with the milkman. It sounds crazy, but it's true."

I turn around then, and he takes a few steps closer. Maybe he doesn't want to shout it. "The milkman gave it to her as a reminder that wherever they were, even if they had nothing else, they had each other...and that was home. And now you have it. Because wherever you are..."

"You're home," I whisper.

"Yeah."

Now I'm ugly-crying and kissing him all over again. I'll be a few minutes late to work. The other professors will understand. They're artists and all artists respect a love story. And that's what me and Tom are becoming. A real love story.

46 CORN DOGS

Nine months later

Brynn

"Is this where you want me?" Tom asks, leaning in.

"Yes..." I whisper, distracted by my need to fondle the object of my desire. "It's so... Long. And so hard."

Tom chuckles. "Honey, I'm glad you like the new countertop, but I'm trying to set up a shoot here."

"It's just that I've never had a stone countertop before." And that's not even my favorite feature of our new kitchen in the Lake Michigan cottage. I have to touch it one more time, so I step over to the sliding door behind me and reveal my very own... Pantry. "Unngh. It's so *big*."

"That's what all the girls say."

"I'm talking about the pantry."

"Me too," he agrees.

I step inside to admire the shelves full of canisters. This is my fantasy right here—five kinds of artisan flour, four types of sugar, each of them waiting in their own canister and properly labeled. There's also a giant bin filled with all-purpose flour. I could bake for days and days, and I just might. A girl could get short of breath just looking at it. I actually am hyperventilating a little.

Tom follows me into the pantry to see what's holding me up. "Honey? Could you take a look at my camera angle? I need your pretty face to get the shot right."

We are about to shoot the first episode of my new web-based cooking show. With Tom's help—and his agent, Patricia's—I got a sweet sponsorship deal.

And? There is no network involved. This is Tom's coup. He says he's done giving up creative control of anything. So he started his own production company, and I'm the first production.

"Let's go, gorgeous." Tom snaps his fingers. "We have twenty-two minutes until we go live. And you're ogling the flour bins again."

"But they are so pretty! Like something Martha would put in one of her magazines."

"Yeah? I'll bet Martha wouldn't have broken-in her kitchen the way you and I did a couple hours ago."

"Mmh. Stop distracting me. We have a show to make." Just remembering our previous activities makes my parts tingle. Nobody breaks in a kitchen like Tom. I will never be able to look at a certain barstool again without getting a little hot, bothered, and dizzy.

My hunk rolls his eyes and beckons me toward the computer screen. We look over the three camera angles he's set up. Everything looks great to me, but he spends a couple of extra minutes reminding me which points along the vast countertop are the most photogenic.

"Hello! Is everybody decent?" It's Sadie's voice in the front hall.

"Of course we are!" I call out. Tom raises his eyebrows at me comically, because if she'd shown up earlier, she would've gotten an eyeful.

"What are you cooking?" she asks, coming into the kitchen with Kate and Amy toddling after her.

"Corn dogs from scratch! It's the perfect beach food." In fact, corndogs have been sold at Lake Michigan for decades—well before food trucks were cool. "It's a wrapped thing that you also dip. Two food groups at once."

"Cool," Sadie says, although we all know that fried foods are a bridge too far for Sadie. She's more of a kale girl. Ah, well. You can lead your friends to junk food, but you can't make them scarf it down.

"And don't worry," she adds. "The girls and I are going for a walk on the beach when you start shooting. We'll come back just in time to taste everything."

"Well, hello there!" Tom says to one of the twins, scooping her up. He cuddles her to his big, strapping chest, and it makes me want to start kissing him all over again.

Focus, Brynn. The countdown timer on the computer says we're going live in nineteen minutes. I need to change into my dressy apron and practice my non-dorky smile.

Tom sets the toddler back on her feet and points at me. "Set up your fry oil. I'll light up the space."

"You already do!" I call back to him. Because it's true. Admittedly, we're a little bit gross right now, but when you're in love like this, it's pretty much expected. Ash and Sadie keep their eye rolls to a minimum, and I ignore Ash when she gags. Speaking of...

The front door bangs open again. I told Tom not to fix it because the screen door at a beach cottage is supposed to bang. That's its job. And I don't have to ask who's come inside, because I'd know Ash's hisses anywhere.

"Listen, dickbag," she says in a threatening voice. "It's not fifty-fifty if I bring in the buyer."

"But you won't, so I don't know why we're even discussing it," Braht counters.

"Hi, friends!" Tom calls out. "We're in the kitchen!"

Ash and Braht enter the kitchen together. Actually, it sort of looks like they're competing to see who can enter the kitchen first, but they end up hip-checking each other to get through the door at the same time. "You are a fucking asshole," she hisses under her breath.

"Language!" Sadie snaps over her shoulder. Her girls will start speaking any day now and she's worried that they'll get their vocabulary from Auntie Ash.

"He started it," my friend says, sounding like a toddler herself.

Braht just beams.

"What's the problem?" I ask, hoping the answer is a brief one. I have a cooking show to make here.

Ash glowers. Really—she does. It's the only word that could possibly describe the scary eyes and the frown that my old friend is throwing off. "*Someone* is trying to renegotiate the standard co-broker agreement."

"It's not standard," Braht argues. "A house of this magnitude requires special attention. The deal is that the sellers' fee is fifty percent, no matter what. Whomever brings in the buyer gets the other half."

"Sounds fair to me," Tom says mildly. Then he winks at me, because he's enjoying this.

And—fine—so am I. It was Tom's idea to give his real estate listing to Ash and Braht together. We really couldn't choose between them, and we thought it might be, I don't know, some fun fireworks to watch. Ash is hysterical when she's pissed off and Braht seems to bring that out of her. You'd think the two of them would be grateful for the easy commission—Tom's house is a stunner, as well as semi-famous.

But Ash and Braht began trying to kill each other about ten seconds after Tom's ink was dry on the listing agreement. Ash sent Tom and me a bottle of champagne as a thank-you gift. But then Braht sent us a magnum of the same vintage, just to show her up.

They've been duking it out ever since.

"Keep it to a dull roar, kids," Tom says, checking his T1 connection for our broadcast. "Find someplace to stand where you can't be seen and also can't reach each other."

"Here I thought twins were tricky," Sadie murmurs.

The rest of our prep time is a blur. My fryer oil is reheating and my ingredients are styled.

"Lookin' good!" Ash cheers from somewhere out of my sight.

I've got nervous butterflies in my tummy. Or maybe that's just the corn dogs I ate while prepping this episode. It's not because I'm afraid to be on camera. It's just that I'm so excited. I didn't know I could have my dream job and my dream guy all at once. Throw in this amazing beach house we're renovating, and I almost have to pinch myself.

"Going live in sixty seconds," Tom says with a smile. He looks so relaxed that it relaxes me too. The lights he set up are warm on my face, but not in a bad way. The moonstone glows on my finger, and the pretty little ramekins where I've arranged my ingredients sparkle. I tie my apron, the equivalent of a cowboy spinning his guns into his holster.

The only worrying thing is the slap I hear from somewhere off set. There's a Braht laugh and a high-pitched growl.

"Omigod, quiet!" I yell.

"Thirty seconds," Tom says. "Ignore them. Look at me, honeybunch."

I do.

He smiles. "Fifteen seconds."

I practice my non-awkward smile. Sadie gives a thumbs up and escorts her girls out the front door so they can dig in the sand for twenty minutes while we film.

"Eight. You look hot, honey. Relax. Three...two...one..."

I smile into the camera and hold it for a count of three, then turn on the heat under my fry oil. Our intro music is fading out now, even though I can't hear it. "Hello, from the beaches of Michigan!" I tell Tom. It's easier to talk to a real person than to try to relate to a camera.

"Thank you for joining me on Brynn's Bites. If it's party food and it's delicious, I'll cook it up for you! Today we're going to make corn dogs and also a sesame-carrot slaw, so we can pretend to care about our health." I gesture at the gorgeous spread of carrots on the countertop. "If you have a thing for corn dogs, I want to hear about it. Email me at this address." I point like Tom told me to, which is weird because I'm pointing at my boobs. He'll fill in the graphic later. "And I'll read some of your comments on next week's show. Now let's get cooking!"

This is fun. I can totally do this, I think. I pick up the cute glass mixing bowl and measure in ingredients, telling my viewers how to stir up a quick batter.

"You know, I think a pinch of sugar makes sense. Let me grab that, and I can show you my new pantry! I'm so excited. I had to come down here and fondle the canisters in the middle of the night. This is where I keep my dry ingredients." I poise my hand on the cut-glass doorknob that Tom chose. "Like dry beans, flours, and baking ingredients such as..."

I whisk the door open.

Several things happen at once. A dust cloud of white bursts from the door. Tom gasps. And a shocking noise vibrates from the rear of the pantry—a deep, primal sound. It's the sound of someone overtaken by...

A knee-quaking orgasm.

Still, my little brain can't quite make sense of this until the dust—my organic flour—settles. And then...

I see Ash and Braht, covered head to toe in flour. They're like two abominable snowmen standing in a pile of...clothes. Because they are naked. Totally naked. Covered in flour. I look down. If Braht really is named after bratwurst, I totally get it, because *damn*.

"Holy...!" I'm officially flailing. *Literally* flailing, and shoving my body in front of the door's opening, hoping the camera angle didn't catch anything juicy.

But, hey, I'm a professional, so I recover rather quickly. "Holy sausage, I love my new pantry!" Maybe that line seems odd, but it's the best I can do. We are live, and it's happening right now, and a girl has to realize that this is a Julia Child moment. *WWJC do?* I face the camera and give a big, crazy smile. "Sugar, please!" I call over my shoulder. "And step on it."

There's the sound of movement behind me, and a canister is placed in my hand.

I slam the pantry door. "Isn't that a great feature!" I babble.

Tom is doubled over with silent laughter, so it's possible we just made another accidental porn flick. It's really surprising how easy it is to do that. Who knew?

"All right," I say, plunking the sugar down and opening the canister. I add the pinch of sugar to my other ingredients and stir up the batter. If I pretend like nothing happened, the lion's share of my viewers might not even notice.

This could go down like that ghost boy behind the curtains in that scene from *Three Men and a Baby*. Weird, but less distracting than you'd think.

Ghost boy. Ghost bratwurst. Same thing?

"Don't overmix!" I say cheerfully. "The buttermilk will activate the baking soda for a *nice rise*."

There are tears rolling down Tom's face now.

"Then you put your wiener on a stick," I say, daring the camera to try it. "Like this." I jam a hot dog onto a wooden skewer and wonder what Braht's wiener is up to in my pantry.

"Dip...twist..." I coat the hot dog with corn-dog batter. "And, fry!"

I slip the first dog into the fryer. The sizzle covers the sound of Tom's hysterical hiccups.

And so it goes. I fry. I make slaw. And, on his side of the counter, Tom sobers up enough that I invite him into the shot as I'm plating the food. "You know who I'm going to share this with, right? Mr. Fixit is here. He built this fab kitchen." I smile at him and beckon.

I can almost hear our live viewership saying "awwww" as Tom steps behind the counter to give me a hug.

"Want the first bite, you big corn dog?" I ask him, holding up a skewer.

"Anytime, anyplace, honeybunch." He gives me a quick kiss that's sure to break hearts. "Anything you make me is my new favorite food."

I hope our viewership is melting, because I surely am.

He picks up another corn dog and hands it to me. We tap them together, as if toasting with glasses of fine champagne. Tom reaches over to tap a button which will play our outro music for the viewers. Then he loops his arm around me and takes another bite.

His computer chimes.

"That's a wrap!" my honey says.

Then we both burst out laughing.

Tom shuts off the lights and folds me into his arms, his Man Hands landing firmly where they belong: on my ass. He's still laughing. And kissing me.

Sadie comes in with the girls and frowns at a trace of flour on the floor outside the pantry. "Uh-oh. Looks like there was an accident."

"Oh, you have no idea!" I say.

"Shut it," a voice says from behind the pantry door. There's some shuffling and then Ash finally opens the door, still completely dusted, but at least dressed.

"Not. One. Word." She smooths her hair. As we all watch, she walks slowly and methodically across the kitchen and to the bathroom.

"She totally hates me," Braht says, emerging from the pantry.

"She does," Tom agrees.

"I'm so into that," Braht says. He grabs a corn dog off the plate.

We all laugh again. Maybe because we're giddy, maybe because it's a stress relief, or maybe because seeing Ash walk past us like the Queen of England after getting groped by Mr. Bratwurst is about as amazing as watching a total eclipse.

Tom leans in and whispers in my ear, "I can't wait to see what you'll cook up next."

"Whatever it is, it'll be an adventure," I say, because that's how my life with Tom is. One adventure after another. Awkward, ridiculous, and beautiful all at once.

"Now we eat!" I announce. It's corn dogs for everyone.

No one—not even Sadie—reaches for the slaw first.

Thank you so much for reading!
Next up: Man Card by Sarina Bowen & Tanya Eby. Get your copy today!

CPSIA information can be obtained
at www.ICGtesting.com
Printed in the USA
LVHW032312061219
639739LV00003B/274/P